"Every chapter of life deserves to be told. Remember that. You're in charge of your own destiny." Her sister pulled her in for a fast sideways hug. She smelled of ink and books with a hint of verbena thrown in. "Don't let anyone tell you otherwise, do you hear me? Write your own story, little sister. Do what makes you happy, and don't listen to anyone else. You know yourself better than anyone ever could…but don't let Mother or Father know I gave that kind of advice." She grinned, and Pansy wished she could keep her sister home with them, even if it were only for a day or two longer.

"I won't." She imagined their parents would frown on such guidance. They, of course, expected her to bow to their wishes and accept their plans for her as indisputable. She hated to see Daisy leave. Out of all her sisters, she felt closest to the daring writer among them. Despite her heart cracking as the stagecoach readied to pull away, she forced a smile onto her face. "Your advice is safe with me." A lump grew in her throat, making it hard to catch a breath. "But I promise, I will do what makes me happy."

Daisy put her arms out and gave her a big hug. She spoke near Pansy's cheek. "And write it all down. Tell your story, sister, because I don't want you to forget any details. Someday we'll be together again, and I'll want to hear all about what you were doing when we were apart."

Praise

"This story by Sarita Leone has it all—beguiling romance, tangled hearts, desperate danger, a princess in need of rescue, and even folks who turn up out of the past. It has the feel of an old-time holiday movie."
~Laura Hartland on *A Wylder Christmas*

"This was a lovely book that put a smile on my face as the story was told to perfection. A great read." ~Dru Love, Dru's Book Musings on *Tip-A-Canoe for Two*

The Wyldest Bloom

by

Sarita Leone

Wylder West Series

The Wyldest Bloom

Cover Art by *Tina Lynn Stout*

The Wild Rose Press, Inc.
PO Box 708
Adams Basin, NY 14410-0708
Visit us at www.thewildrosepress.com

Publishing History
First Edition, 2024
Trade Paperback ISBN 978-1-5092-5218-3
Digital ISBN 978-1-5092-5134-6

Wylder West Series
Published in the United States of America

Dedication

For Vito, always.
Sempre per sempre

Chapter 1

Charleston, South Carolina
October 1879

Pansy stared at the familiar word as the blood in her veins turned to ice.

BLOOM

Stark and harsh, the massive letters centered on the gray granite headstone held no warmth despite the day's oppressive heat. She sucked in air that burned all the way to her lungs as the words beneath her surname tore a hole in her heart, the chisel marks so fresh they looked sharp enough to cut a finger. Her gaze rested on the inscription while her mind searched for clarity.

Henrietta Elizabeth Beloved Wife and Mother
Daniel Edward Beloved Husband and Father
Died together on September 22, 1879
Their love could not keep them safe from the dreadful pox
Side by side in eternal repose

It came as a terrible ending to a love story that had influenced so many others. Her parents were pillars of their South Carolinian community, a genteel couple who were the epitome of graceful living. Her father's law practice had been hugely successful, and Mother's benevolence to causes she deemed worthy elevated many lives. Together they raised a family, supported local businesses, been an integral part of polite society, both before and following the war. They had made a difference in Charleston, and now that they were gone, many would feel the loss.

Pansy's heart hurt. They did not deserve to die this way.

Their final days, feverish, wracked by delirium, calling out in hoarse voices for each other as well as the long-dead son they'd lost at Chancellorsville. Heartbreaking to hear and not be able to satisfy their wishes. The memory of their cries would haunt her forever.

The hours when the doctor tended her parents while she bathed their failing bodies with cool, lavender-scented water were a waste. A horrible, agonizing time when no amount of prayer or care could change the outcome.

Their pained groans echoed in the hallways of the grand house. With the passing hours, they grew fainter, until they came no more.

A tragedy. A love story cut short by an insidious ailment. Several in the city had been lost before the sickness ran its course. Others spared. It made no sense, but logic did not matter now. It did not soothe a shattered heart.

The only consolation, that they departed this world within moments of each other.

She stared at the stone and vowed to never fall in love. She'd always dreamed of love like her parents had found, but now that she'd seen the heartache that kind of devotion brought, she decided to forgo the whole affair.

Spinsterhood beckoned, and she would rather walk into that lifestyle than spend her final moments calling out to one who would never again reply. She'd seen the brutality of true love. It was not for her.

A hand came around her shoulders. Her dearest friend from childhood, Emmaline Birch, pulled her into a side hug. The safe, solid presence of one who'd known her since they were mere babies brought comfort.

"I'm so sorry. This shouldn't be happening." Emmaline, with her blonde curls and well-endowed figure, had the countenance of an angel. Now she gave Pansy's shoulder a squeeze and placed her other hand over her own chest. "It just breaks my heart to lose your parents this way. Why, they were hardly old enough to pass. My parents are older than yours, and they're still strong. Yours should be, too."

They had been, until they took sick. While they'd never fully recovered from losing their only son in the war, they had found a way to be happy again. Content, and involved in Charlestonian life. With her three older sisters living out west, she and her parents had grown very close. They were all any of them had. And now, she had nothing.

The family property and most of its contents had sold almost before she could bury her parents. What few items she wanted to keep were stored over at the Birch's place, in a section of one of their outbuildings that they weren't using. A blessing, to leave the remnants of their lives in a safe location for now. Maybe for a long while, really.

"I agree." Her parents shouldn't be lying side by side in matching coffins beneath the loamy South Carolinian soil. They should be back in their home, walking the grounds and discussing current events over endless pots of Earl Grey tea. A small smile at the memory of the tiny crack on the teacup Mother favored. She'd wrapped it carefully before sending it to storage with the Birches.

She shook the image of her parents in their funeral finery from her head. It wouldn't do to dwell on what could not be changed. And as much as she missed them, she could not bring them back from the dead.

Pansy turned from the gravestone and gazed out across the rolling acreage. Magnolia Cemetery appeared almost like a park. That is, if you didn't pay too much attention to the grave markers, wooden crosses, and flowers in glass jars.

Her family had bought one of the first plots in the place, for their son lost in battle and the family that would eventually need a resting place, so the decision to inter her parents here took no effort. Their wishes, really, to be buried near her brother. She was only carrying out the plan they had set in motion.

Any plans after this one were all hers. No one to discuss anything with or to turn to for counsel. Every single decision she made from here going forward fell on her shoulders. The weight of it all made her stagger, but she refused to be buried by it.

Too many Blooms were already dug in, she thought. She glanced at the headstones. Nearly half of the family, underground.

A whip-poor-will chortled from a low-hanging branch of a nearby weeping willow. She stared into its glossy black eye, wondering if it sang for the dead or the living. No way to know which he chose, but the song soothed her nerves a bit.

Mother always said that when a whip-poor-will chanted near a home, it meant a death would surely befall the family soon. Death had already claimed her loved ones, so she brushed aside the folksy wisdom and imagined it came not as a harbinger of death but new beginnings.

Time to turn nearly all the beliefs she'd held her whole life on their edge. This starting over point had to come on her terms, not from what was but with the possibility of what might be. Someday, anyhow. Once she got out of town for good, that is.

She gave the bird one last look before she turned to the other woman. "You will come by and check on them, won't you? My brother, too?"

Pansy didn't think she'd ever return to this spot, not even when she had breathed her last breath. She had no idea where she would spend her final days, but she didn't intend to live them in South Carolina. Too many heartaches here for her to come back. It would remain part of her, this place where she'd lived the first twenty-two years of her life, but it would not claim another year of her existence.

Time to move on.

"You know I will. Why, my kin are buried here, too." Emmaline pointed toward a spot nearer the pond, where her family owned a parcel of land. An aunt and two uncles occupied the space, but eventually the rest of the family would join them. "You know Father bought that huge piece so we could all stay together, to rest in peace within reaching distance of each other." She placed a hand over her lips and giggled. "Although I doubt I'll be doing any reaching at that point, but we keep him happy, don't we?"

Mr. Birch had returned from the war somewhat addle-minded. While everyone who knew the man felt gratitude for his homecoming, those closest to him spent a good deal of time and energy keeping him from making a spectacle of himself. They succeeded, mostly.

"It is a small thing, to keep your father happy." Pansy shot a look over her shoulder toward the fresh graves. "I would give anything to be able to cater to Father one more time." A tear escaped and rolled down her cheek, hot and wet. She'd cried so many, it seemed impossible there were any left to shed.

"I'm so sorry. I'm being insensitive." Emmaline pulled her into a sisterly hug, so she let her face drop to her friend's shoulder. Nice, to have one to cry on. After today that consideration would be gone from her life, so she gave in and sobbed.

A kind hand patted her back, the way Mother would have done had she been here. It hit her that she'd never again feel her mother's touch, and the anguish that came with the realization nearly dropped her to her knees.

She had to stop crying. If she didn't, she would be lost forever. Trapped in a soul-sucking grief that would define the rest of her days. It would be a waste of her life, a loss to add to the ones lying nearby. Gone before their time, and she would be, too, unless she caught hold of herself.

Her back straightened, and she turned from her friend's warm embrace. The lace hanky tucked inside her cuff tidied up her face. Her eyes felt puffy, but there was no help for it.

A sniff. She offered a shaky smile. "You are kind, Emmaline. I am grateful for your friendship, and I will not forget you."

The other woman grabbed her wrist, a shocked expression on her face. Creamy skin and wide blue eyes, framed by golden ringlets, gave her a delicate air, but that deception led others to think her weak when she most certainly was not. Her strength showed itself now in the determined glare she leveled at Pansy.

"Don't you ever even consider forgetting me! We have been like sisters almost from birth, and I could not imagine life without you." She gasped, and her voice shook, but her stare didn't waver. "I can hardly believe you're actually leaving Charleston. Why, you know you can come stay with my family if you want. Mother and Father think of you as one of their own already."

The offer had been extended several times, but Pansy would not remain in the city. The only living Bloom in what was once their happy place, the foundation of their family? She couldn't do it.

Better to leave and find a new life.

"I will never forget you." She removed her wrist with a gentle tug and put her hand on the other's slender shoulder. "And when I am settled, I will write you and ask you to visit me. We will laugh again, I promise." She shot a look at the graves, then met her friend's blue-eyed gaze. "I only know that if I don't get out of this place, I shall surely go mad. Please, understand that I have to leave."

****

The only other leave-taking she needed to do mattered less than walking from her parents' graves or Emmaline's companionship. Pansy considered catching a stagecoach out of the city without saying a word to Filbert Snowe, but he deserved better.

Besides, she'd never been intentionally mean and wasn't about to begin now.

The trees lining the walkway in the small park where

they often strolled in the evenings after he left off work at his father's accounting firm provided some shade. A row of old oaks, so strong and straight they reminded her of easier times, like those before the war came upon the south. But the leaves remained still, as if locked in rigor mortis, and offered no breeze at all.

A bead of perspiration trailed down her spine. Black mourning dresses, even those made of cotton, were hot and heavy, and hers was no exception. A corset cut into her tender skin, tied so tightly it barely left room for her to breathe.

Best to get straight to the heart of things. Then, she could return to Emmaline's for one last night in the city. Her coach left in the morning, and she couldn't wait to escape the dry, hot air that surrounded her.

But first, to sever this last association.

They'd met at the park entrance, beneath the wrought-iron gate that welcomed visitors. The lane had few other strollers at this time, so they walked slowly. So far, they'd only exchanged pleasantries. A few moments to gather the courage to say what needed saying had stretched into several silent minutes.

Time to plunge in.

"Filly, we need to talk." She planned to be firm with him. No wiggle room, no way for him to dissuade her. He had a tendency to steer her over to his way of thinking, and in the past she'd allowed him to do so, merely to save herself the effort of debating trivial issues with the man. But this time, there would be little, if any, discussion.

Her mind was made up.

"Yes, we do." He placed his free hand over hers where it rested on his arm. They walked a respectable distance from each other, but close enough that when he offered his arm, as he did every time they strolled, she took it. "Why don't we sit on that bench? It is too hot to be traipsing through the park."

Finally, something they agreed on. Black wrought-iron benches placed along the lane provided places to rest. She sat when they reached the nearest and waited for him to settle onto the sun-warmed seat beside her.

Pansy fanned her face with one hand. It would have been so much easier if she'd just left the city without seeing him. "I need to tell you something, and I'm not sure you'll like it. I'm sorry, though, my mind is set, so please don't try to talk me out of it."

Her companion draped an arm across the back of the bench. Attractive in an ordinary sort of way, he had features that were neither handsome nor horrid. Eyes, brown. Hair the color of mud. Nose and mouth both forgettable. Nothing about the man made him stand out in a crowd, which of course couldn't be helped. Now he smiled, showing straight teeth and the friendly disposition that first attracted her to him.

"Of course, I won't try to change your resolve about anything. You know your own mind. You don't need any help from anyone." He flashed her a grin before he went on. "But before you tell me your news, I hope you'll listen to mine."

Just like him, she thought. Turning the table and taking charge, all with a smile and a few well-chosen, bland phrases. Fine. Let him have his moment.

It would be the last evening she'd have to listen to him. Or give him the opportunity to cut in when she wanted to speak.

"Certainly, Filly." A swallow to conceal her

annoyance at his being so pushy. She forced a smile. "What's on your mind?"

She hoped whatever occupied his thoughts came in a rush and left as quickly. Her parched throat could do with a refreshing glass of lemonade, and since she and Emmaline had squeezed a dozen lemons barely an hour earlier, she knew just where to find that relief.

"Well, it's more of what's in my heart." He shifted, bringing his arm down and moving toward the edge of the bench. "I could kick myself for not doing this before the pox hit your home, but done is done. I've given this a lot of thought, and I need to ask you a very important question."

Her heart stuttered in her chest. Suddenly her corset seemed too tight for her to catch a breath.

Oh, holy hell. He couldn't be doing what she thought, could he?

When the man reached into his broadcloth jacket and pulled out a ring box, her stomach sank into her shoes.

Pansy's mind screamed for her to run, but she remained frozen.

Filly turned his lips up in a hopeful smile and opened the box. Inside, an opal ring.

She couldn't let him ask. It wouldn't be fair to hear the words pass his lips, not when she knew her answer wouldn't be favorable.

Her lips were suddenly dry. She touched her tongue to the lower, but it, too, had become like the desert. "Filly, please, let me tell you what I need to say."

Of course, he cut her off. "But Pansy, I'm trying to ask you—"

She pressed on, fueled by the erratic beating in her

chest and the overwhelming desire to be away from the man and his ring. "I know, but I need to tell you something first—"

He held a hand up between them. His cheeks were red, and the dull brown eyes flashed. She had never seen him frustrated before now. It did not increase his appeal in the slightest.

"Pansy Mae Bloom, I don't know what you're all-fired up to say, but I'm trying to ask you something mighty important here." His tone showed his anger. "You seem determined to interrupt me, and I can't see why that is when all I'm doing is asking you to—"

She raised her own hand and sliced it through the air in front of his face. Had he leaned forward a bit, she may have skimmed the tip of his nose. "I'm leaving Charleston in the morning." When he stared at her as if she'd lost her mind, she added, "Filbert Emmanuel Snowe, I'm leaving with first light and don't intend to return."

His mouth dropped open.

She looked away and wondered how on earth to shut a man's mouth. She'd stopped the river of words that had gushed forth, but now he looked as befuddled as a carp left drying in the sun on a splintered dock.

A minute, maybe. That's what he needed to regain his wits. Women rarely took more than a few breaths before being able to resume a conversation, so how much different could a man be? Sure, she thought. She'd give him a minute, and he'd recover his mind.

The leaves above them remained stubbornly still. More than ever, she wished for a drink to slake her thirst. It would come soon, now that she'd dealt with this final obligation.

A deep breath before she turned to meet the man's astonished gaze. He'd managed to close his mouth but still looked at her as if she'd gone mad.

"Are you serious?"

A nod. "I am."

He waved the small box toward her. The opal caught the sun's rays and sparkled. "But I have a ring. You're supposed to marry me." He waved the offering a second time. "Don't you understand? That's the plan, for you to take the ring and marry me."

She sighed. Her whole life others had presumed to make plans for her. Why should she expect anything different now?

First, her parents. That she understood, up to a point. Even when she'd grown old enough to think for herself, they'd insisted on running her life. She'd allowed it, although she hated being such a soft touch.

Her sisters. Lord, but they had thought her incapable of coming up with one intelligent idea on her own. They'd bossed her about right up until the time they'd left for a place called Wylder, in the Wyoming territory. She missed them, but not their overbearing dictates about what concerned her.

Even her dearest friend, when she was of a mood, decided what they would do. Shopping or seeing a play? Strolling in the park or reading on the front porch of either of their homes? Leave it to her friend to decide, because of course she knew nothing and everyone, including Emmaline, knew better.

And now this man stared at her as if he couldn't believe she had an idea in her head, one that didn't fall in line with the plans he'd so presumptuously made for her.

For her whole life, even! If she agreed now, she'd be stuck with the man for every day that remained to her. She'd be at his beck and call, catering to his needs, running his household, and doing God only knew what else. She'd heard stories…she wasn't as naïve as he probably thought. Her virtue remained intact, but that didn't mean she lived beneath an overturned milk can.

Time to end this. Cut the tie, break the bond, leave the man to his ring and his delusions. Why, they'd never even kissed. What made him think she'd marry him?

Self-centered, she thought. He thought only of what he wanted with no regard for her feelings.

Well, she had her own mind and wasn't afraid to use it. Not anymore. Her parents' deaths had freed her from the obligation to allow others to determine her actions.

"I'm leaving tomorrow. It's been, ah, pleasant knowing you, and I wish you well." Pansy stood and smoothed a hand down the front of her skirt. She couldn't wait to get back to Emmaline's so she could shimmy out of it and into a lightweight wrapper. "I can see myself home."

She took two steps before he spoke. When he did, she remembered her manners and turned to face him.

"You're just grieving, is all. When you come to your senses, you'll see this is the only solution to your problem and you'll thank me for giving you this way out." He jabbed the jeweler's box in the air between them as if he brandished a weapon.

Her brow furrowed. "I assure you my senses are intact. You're the one who seems to have difficulty thinking." She paused when she realized her voice grew louder with each word. No need to attract undue attention. In the last few minutes, others had come into the park, and many were walking the lane. "What problem is it that I supposedly have? And the way out of what?"

Filbert Snowe stood, and she realized for the first time that his lankiness could also be imposing. The man stepped close. He leaned forward and lowered his voice, speaking so only she could hear. "Your problem? Why, you are a woman alone, on your own with no one to care for you. No one to support you or defend you. Pansy, you are at the mercy of the world." He raised the ring box so it came between them at chest level. The opal sat in the shadows their bodies cast and didn't sparkle at all. She peered down at the shaded stone and saw only darkness. Nothing to bring joy, only a cold, hard stone that would seal her fate forever. "This is your way out of a life of misery, of spinsterhood, a lonely, forgotten existence."

His words sent heat dancing off her skin in waves. If he'd thought to shock her into submission, he'd misjudged.

She raised her gaze to his and forced a smile to her lips. A look born from anger, not happiness. Purely for show, to leave the man with the memory that his harsh treatment and condemning words could not break her. She would not shed a tear for him and most certainly not in front of him.

"I'm going to give you the courtesy of a reply because I don't want any misunderstanding between us." She inhaled so deeply the sash on her skirt dug into her waist. "I would rather be at the mercy, as you put it, of the world than in your bed. I greatly prefer the idea of spinsterhood over having to listen to you for the rest of my life."

His cheeks reddened, and his eyes bulged. "How can

you say that? We had an understanding—"

"*You* had an understanding. I had no part in any of this." She tilted her head, the smile on her face growing as his mouth dropped open again. "And just so we're clear, you're wrong. I am not in a position that either looks or hopes for mercy. Not from you, the world, or anyone. I am perfectly capable of thinking and caring for myself, and I fully intend to do just that." She straightened her spine and brought herself to her full height. A small woman, she could never hope to intimidate a man, but the feel of her shoulders pulled back and her chest pushed out gave her a boost. "And if I do end up a spinster, it will be because during the course of my life I will have only met ordinary, self-serving men like you. If that is the case, which I sincerely hope it won't be, I will choose spinsterhood over marriage, the way I'm choosing to venture forth on my own over sheltering in your arms."

Pansy sucked in one more deep breath, then released it in a slow, satisfying whoosh.

The man stood as still as if he'd been turned to stone like one of the statues in Magnolia Cemetery. Those, at least, were heartwarming while his vapid stare and wide-mouthed astonishment sickened her.

She sighed. "Close your mouth, Filly. You'll attract a fly if you're not careful."

Chapter 2

Pansy settled back against the seat in the carriage and watched as she passed familiar sights. The place she'd been born and raised, now a blur from within the conveyance. She should have felt more, she thought, but she didn't. No matter how hard she tried to pull heartfelt emotion over leaving, she could not muster one bit. Not one tear, either.

She supposed she'd shed all the tears in her in the last weeks.

As she watched the streets pass, she felt certain she would never return. She'd promised friends and neighbors that she would be back, but that had been a lie. Every time it passed her lips, she knew the truth but kept a grin pasted on her face. Sometimes she wondered if those who smiled back also realized her dishonesty. They probably did but had the good southern grace to not let on.

Were there streetcars like this one in the west? She supposed not, but her idea of life past the Mississippi did not include many facts or details gleaned from those who had been there. Most folks she knew who traveled west did not return east.

Like her sisters. All three had gone toward the frontier and never come back to Charleston again. They'd all headed out, and aside from letters, they cut all ties with their original home.

Violet left first to become a bride to a man she knew only from correspondence. To Pansy's way of thinking, it seemed a strange means to form a union, but her sister assured her she wanted to go settle with the man. And there were a lot of mail-order brides going west, so why not join them?

Unfortunately, when she arrived in Wylder, Violet learned her intended had died. But the good news, that he left his house and possessions to her, made it easy for her to settle in town.

Lily and Daisy…well, their leaving had almost been necessary to save Lily's reputation. She'd been betrothed to a local man, a womanizer and good-for-nothing with a rich family. His proposal assured her sister of a life of abundance, if not love. As the eldest and nearing the time when she'd be considered past her bloom, Lily jumped at the chance. Pansy suspected it had more to do with her sister not wanting to be a spinster than caring for the man, but since no one asked her opinion on the matter, she kept her mouth shut. When the nuptials were called off, her sister left town. She headed west, to Wylder and Violet.

Daisy went off with Lily, more to get out on her own than anything else. She made no secret of the fact that she didn't intend to get married, preferring a solitary life of writing. Her passion was her pen, and the only stories she needed came from her own head. Of all her sisters, Pansy admired their author the most.

But like Violet, neither Daisy nor Lily returned home after they'd gone.

Now, her turn to wipe the memories of Charleston from her mind and find a new adventure for herself. Time to live her life as it suited her, without anyone telling her what to do or think. Time to…

But God, did she miss her parents. Their kindness and care, and even the way they nudged her into doing what they thought right. It came as part of being a parent, didn't it, to guide offspring into living a life that would bring them health and happiness?

She saw both views. Their loving concern for her, so much more all-encompassing after the others had gone. And her desire to think for herself, to carve her own way. Unfortunate that they had never found a better balance between them, that she'd felt squashed beneath their expectations and rules. Now that they were gone, this liberation came as a relief, but it also had a level of terror that accompanied it.

What if she couldn't make her way in the world on her own? Suppose all her ideals and plans were rubbish, and she fell flat on her face in a place where she knew no one, where not a single soul cared about her?

No, she couldn't think that way. If she were to be so doubtful at this point, how would she ever make her way anywhere? She wouldn't, that's what. Stuck in a hole of her own making, wanting to rule the course of her life but afraid to grab the reins. It wouldn't do.

A bundle of letters accompanied her on this trek. Ties to her sisters, they had been read so many times the paper had softened. She pulled the white glove from her right hand and reached inside the bag beside her to slide one envelope from beneath the lavender ribbon that held them together.

The familiar handwriting settled the thumping in her chest before she even read one word.

August 25, 1879
My sweet Pansy,

I hope this finds you and our dear parents well. Even though there is a distance between us, you all remain close in my heart. I know I speak for Violet and Lily, too. We all miss you, little sister.

Since you've never been out of Charleston and I have no idea when, or if, you'll ever see the western frontier, I shall continue telling you all about life in the wild west. I say that with a smile, because this west is not so wild that I want you to worry. Lily, Violet, and I are all safe in our sister's small lavender house. I still smile every day when I walk up to the door and see she's painted it this shade. Mother would love it, secretly I think, but counsel that it might not be seemly for a woman to paint a house the color of candy.

You asked about cowboys in your last letter. Yes, there are cowboys here, and we see them daily. The ones who come off the trail are dusted with trail grime. They wear bandanas, and if the wind kicks up or they find themselves in the middle of a storm, they pull them up to cover the bottom of their sun-chiseled features. They are a strong bunch, wearing spurs and leather vests, with hats pulled low over their faces. I've not had close dealings with any, but if I pass one on Wylder Street or even near the livery and our gazes meet, there's a level of politeness I wouldn't have expected. A tip of the head, or a nod, but I've never felt unsafe when I meet a cowboy.

Of course, none of us go out after dark. And, regardless of the time of day, we steer clear of the saloon. Yes, there's an actual saloon here, with swinging batwing doors. Nothing like the Gentleman's Club on Greene Street in Charleston, I'll say that much.

But let's not linger on cowboys. Or the Five Star. That's the saloon, by the way. But don't tell Mother I spoke of it.

You know that Violet has a Chinese woman living here. Her name is Lin, and she is the kindest woman I've ever met—aside from Mother, that is. Her English is improving, and the more she knows how to speak with us, the more we learn about China. I imagine she misses her home the way I sometimes miss Charleston. But then there are other times when I feel as if I've lived in Wylder my whole life, and I wonder if Lin feels that way, too. In any event, it is a rare treat to have such a person with us. I never thought I'd meet anyone from China in my lifetime, yet we shelter beneath the same roof inside these lavender walls.

It just shows that anything is possible, little sister.

Well, that's all for now. Lily will be griping soon that I need to blow out the candle and go to sleep. She's still bossy. We may be in this new frontier, but some things simply do not change.

Stay well. Love to Mother and Father.

Your sister,

Daisy

Daisy's letters brought Wylder to life. Her writing talent let Pansy glimpse the place in her mind's eye, which had both good and bad sides to it. She yearned to see a cowboy for herself and would love to meet the Chinese Lin, but there had to be a lot that her sister held back. The place was called the wild west, not the tame west, after all. It couldn't be all gentlemanly nods and shopping at the mercantile.

Daisy said that anything was possible, but there were times when that, too, sounded hollow. With little funds, no home, prospects, or direction, how could anything at all be possible? In this moment everything seemed impossible—or at least, improbable. The future looked bleak, and that truth couldn't be denied.

A tear rolled down her cheek, so she turned her head toward the window and caught it on a fingertip. She looked down at her wet skin, the salty water covering the swirls on the tip of her finger. So, she did have a tear or two left inside her, but they weren't for Charleston, her parents, or the life she left behind.

They were for herself and the fear she wasn't woman enough to face whatever lay before her.

Pansy swallowed around the lump in her throat and willed her eyes to dry. A sniff, then she turned her attention to the landscape. She straightened her spine, pressed her shoulders down, and set her lips in a tight, straight line. Whatever the world had in store for her, she planned to meet it head on. Rise to every challenge and build a life worth living.

On her terms. And without anyone else's opinion of what she should think, say, or do.

Time to grow up. Become her own woman.

See that some things were possible, even for an orphan trying to find her way in an uncertain world. She would do it, even if it took every ounce of resolve she possessed.

I can do this, she thought as she they chugged past a long stretch of pastureland. Whatever happens, I'll figure it out. On my own.

****

Train travel was much less glamorous than Pansy imagined. Hot, dirty, and noisy, whereas she'd expected elegant, relaxing, and sweet-smelling.

The truth did not fill any of those and proved to be much further from her dream than she cared to admit, even to herself.

When horse-drawn streetcars came to Charleston, she had pestered her father to allow her to ride the new mode of transportation. She and Emmaline had watched the sandy soil being excavated and speculated on how smoothly wheels would roll over the metal tracks. Even if the streetcars didn't make them feel as if they were flying above the dusty streets, it had to be an improvement over bumping along the rutted soil. Their speculations grew as the shiny rails went down, so by the time the first rides were offered, they were adamant that they ride. But Father had reservations, being a prudent sort, and thought it an unnecessary risk to take with the last of his offspring remaining at home.

Luckily, she'd grown up watching her sisters and mother wheedling what they wanted from him, so she put on the daughterly charm. A few "Yes, Father's" and demure head nods when he advised that she and Emmaline not travel in a coach with men. Only women, he insisted, could be trusted to keep to the genteel nature he expected to surround his daughters.

So, the pair gained entry to the newfangled type of travel and, truth be known, took every opportunity to ride the railed coaches. Like gliding on water, Emmaline proclaimed.

Now her friend's voice echoed in her head as Pansy's behind smacked against the burgundy leather seat beneath her. How a train could bump so vigorously came as a mystery, but this Union Pacific railroad car bucked like a mule. It certainly did not bear much resemblance to the wonderful streetcars.

She'd been raised to endure what couldn't be changed, and since she didn't feel like walking out west, she gritted her teeth and set her concentration on other ideas. Musings like where she planned to end up, what she intended to do when she arrived, and how she expected to live the rest of her life on her own.

There were no answers to any of those questions. When she considered them, it seemed more likely that the train would fly from the tracks than she would find solutions to even one of the issues that traveled with her. Despite yearning for the freedom to make up her own mind about what concerned her, when it came right down to it, she had not been prepared to do so. No one instructed her on the mechanics of decision-making, and it came bundled in all kinds of worry.

The world waited, yet she had no substantial plans for herself. Worse, she wasn't sure how to make them.

I wish Mother were here. She'd know what I should do.

No time to worry. Whatever happened, she'd figure out a way to move forward.

Now, to read another of the letters. They were like balm to her nervous soul. She reached into her bag and slid one from the bundle. The handwriting on the envelope, so straight and precise, gave the writer's identity away. No one wrote with as fine a hand as her schoolteacher sister, Violet. She pulled the single sheet out and unfolded it.

December 10, 1878

Dear Pansy,

It is with deep affection that I write this letter. I pray Mother, Father, and you are all keeping healthy. And warm, certainly warm. Oh, how I recall with fondness the warmth of our southern home. Even on the chilliest days of winter, we were not subjected to freezing temperatures and driven snow. That's right, here the snow is considered driven as if by horses because it blows so hard. I have never seen anything like it.

How I long for home right now. I would not return, I have a good life here and I am content, but I do miss all the festivities. In Charleston, there are parties and decorations everywhere. In Wylder, they are here, but they are more subtle. A spray of pine boughs on a door. The scent of sweet bread wafting on the chilly air. Peppermints in a bowl on the counter at the mercantile.

Frontier life is different than what we grew up knowing, dear sister. The land is unforgiving, and that makes folks tougher, I think. I've seen women do the work of men and not even look as if they're put off by it. There's an acceptance that out here the land and its dangers, both natural and man-made, dictate life.

But I don't want you to have the wrong idea about this place or the life I'm leading. It's not bad, just different. And in the differences, I am finding joy and growth.

I love my job at the schoolhouse. My pupils are preparing for the Christmas Eve festivities. Well, we are still in the planning stages, but when it comes to schoolchildren, that planning becomes preparation, as well. We will offer the townsfolk food, games, a visit from Santa, who is really the sheriff in disguise. The children will sing, and gifts will be handed out. All in all, it should be a night to remember.

Well, as much as I hate to do so, I must sign off. Morning comes early out here, and I will leave for the schoolhouse before dawn. So much to do and very little help.

Please give my love to Mother and Father. And save

some for yourself, sweet Pansy.
Love,
Violet

Violet had a way with words. Her letters were different from Daisy's but no less entertaining. She did not embellish a story the way their writer sister did. But she gave facts that the other did not. A nice balance, receiving news from both.

"Well, look at this. Two lonely travelers."

Her reflections were interrupted by the sound of a male voice. It came from behind, so she looked up and over her shoulder. A man stood in the aisle, a black tweed carpetbag in one hand and a brown bowler hat in the other. He smiled, showing one gold tooth.

With a motion toward the empty seat across from her, he asked, "Mind if I sit a spell?"

A northerner. The accent gave him away, and being the to-the-bone southern belle she was, it crossed Pansy's mind to deny him the privilege of sitting close to her. But the train held a crowd, bringing nearly every car to near capacity, so how could she refuse the man? Besides, if she made him leave, he might cause a scene, and surely she could live without that.

A nod of her head brought a wider smile to the stranger's face. He tipped his head, stowed his bag in the compartment above the seats, then sat. For a long moment neither spoke. He did not hide the fact that he stared, or that he inspected every inch of her. The man's gaze swept from the tips of her sturdy black traveling shoes up to her hat. They rested once or twice on areas of her body, but she resisted the urge to wriggle beneath his scrutiny.

Damn impudent of him, but she still did not wish to

bring attention to herself, so she bit her tongue and turned her gaze away. Perhaps if she ignored the cad, he might leave off inspecting her as if she were an insect on the end of one of his northern fingertips.

The view outside the window showed a dismal scene. A stretch of ramshackle buildings with broken glass in the windows and doors hanging open offered little by way of interest or entertainment, but she focused on the lonely sights and ignored the fellow traveler.

She heard him huff once or twice, as if trying to call attention to himself. Well, if he thought she turned for every man who breathed too loudly, he surely had misjudged her. Her focus remained on the scenery.

He cleared his throat. "Well, looks like we're traveling companions. And a prettier one I couldn't ask for."

Pansy finally turned her head to face the man. She gave him a small smile but wished he had chosen a different seat. Would it be impolite to get up and change her own spot? Certainly it would be, and perhaps be the scene-starter she wished to avoid, so she took a deep breath and gave him a tiny nod.

Just one nearly imperceptible jut of her chin to her chest, and the man took off like a shot.

"Well, it's a fine state of things when a man finds himself paired up with a gentlewoman like yourself. Tell me, ma'am, where are you comin' from?"

While she couldn't say precisely why she didn't want to reveal anything about herself to the newcomer, she felt compelled to fabricate the details of her life. Why on earth should she divulge the true nature of her person to this northerner?

"Atlanta."

He raised an appraising eyebrow. "Atlanta? In Georgia?"

"The very same, of course."

A minute of silence, when all that met her ears came from the rumble of metal wheels over well-worn track. A blessing, to not hear the man's annoying accent.

Father said that one of the worst sounds he'd ever heard had been the battle cry of a northern general. She'd never forgotten her father's aversion to the memory, and now she understood why he'd been so adamant his daughters not interact with those who opposed the south.

"Well, I'm from Boston. You know, I'm sure, about Boston." He grinned, showing the tooth again. "We're responsible for the original colonies. Well, without us there wouldn't be any wild west. No south, either. Well, you all owe us for your way of life, I reckon. Even if the south did need a bit of correctin'."

Just when she thought she would scream if he used the word "well" one more time, he had the audacity to insult the south. Pansy set her lips in a tight, hard line so that she didn't disgrace her mother's memory by telling this cabbage-brained sorry excuse for a man exactly what she thought of him. He and his damned Boston could jump right into the cold, stormy Atlantic Ocean for all she cared.

Her blood heated, and she felt her cheeks flush.

Count to ten. Remember Mother and count before you say something so unladylike she'll be rolling in her grave.

Pansy counted. Twice.

Then she stood, grabbed her traveling satchel, and stepped out into the aisle.

She wouldn't give him the satisfaction of seeing

he'd rattled her.

The man reached out a hand to grab her arm, but she pulled it beyond his reach.

"Well, where are you off to? We're not near any stop on the line, and well, I thought we'd have plenty of time to get to know each other better." He waggled two bushy brown eyebrows at her, reminding her of a pair of caterpillars scuttling across a tree limb.

"*Well*—" She intentionally drew the word out in mockery of his excessive use of it. "I do believe I know you as well as I'd like to. My location on this train is what needs *a bit of correcting*. Good day, sir."

The man didn't let her go without some bluster. He stood and turned as she stepped away. His voice rose when he called after her. "Well, I must've been misinformed. I'd been told southern women were charming."

The hairs on the back of her neck stood on end. She should have kept walking, but his insult struck a nerve that zinged through her like a bolt of lightning. During the war, her mother and sisters worked at the makeshift hospital where wounded soldiers fought for their lives. Sometimes they were charged with caring for northern soldiers, men like this brazen one. They'd saved northern lives, and now she did not deserve—nor would she accept—such disrespect.

She turned on the heel of one shoe and stopped in the aisle. His outburst had caught the attention of other travelers, but she didn't care. The time for worrying about creating a scene had come and gone.

The train chugged on steadily, bumping over tracks so that she swayed from side to side. Her hip hit the unforgiving metal frame of the seat beside her, but she didn't flinch. A stare, long and hard, for the man, before she did him the honor of speaking to him.

"Southern women are smart enough to know better than to waste an ounce of charm on a dog. And you, sir, make the mangiest canine look like a prince."

She turned and walked toward the front of the car, conscious of the snickering and whispering breaking out behind her. When she'd nearly reached the door at the end of the car, a man stood and motioned toward the empty seat across from his.

"I'd be honored, ma'am, if you'll sit near me." His voice held a tinge of that familiar southern drawl she loved so dearly. His tone offered something else, as well. Kindness in the face of adversity, something of great value. "I promise I have never intentionally insulted a lady." He raised his voice. "And I am not now, nor have I ever been, a dog wearing men's clothing."

She brought a hand to cover her mouth. The giggle could not be suppressed, so she didn't try to hide her amusement.

A fast look back at the northern man, whose red-faced anger made him even less appealing. Then, she glanced up into the eyes of one of the handsomest men she'd ever seen.

Something low in her gut flipped—or flopped, she couldn't be sure which, and it certainly didn't matter. The attraction she felt surprised her so much that all thoughts left her head for an instant. Finally, she nodded.

"I would like that very much, sir."

She slipped onto the seat across from his and offered a grateful smile when he took his own again.

"I'm glad you decided to sit with me." He waved a hand to the ink-smudged newspaper spread across the seat beside him. "The news is dreadfully dull. I confess, I was close to snoring when I heard the exchange between yourself and, ah, your friend."

"I assure you, he's no friend of mine." She shrugged one shoulder. "And I apologize if I woke you."

"Oh, I'm very happy you did. Why, the whole train ride has just taken a turn for the better."

****

Clive Cooper wasn't one to moon over a woman. The opposite, in fact. They were nice to look at and surely had their place in society, but that didn't include hanging on either of his arms.

His arms needed to be free and ready to slide his Colts from their holsters in less time than it took a man's heart to beat. That instant, the half-second pause in the beat of an ordinary heart, gave him the chance to do what he did best: kill. And men weren't easy to take down when you had a female dripping off your elbow like some bit of finery that'd been left out in a rainstorm.

And that's how he'd felt about women all these long years since the end of the war. Every man he'd cared for or looked up to had gone to fight, and most didn't return home. From where he stood, it made no sense. They'd all marched off, rifles on their shoulders and chests puffed with pride, to defend the southern way of living, to protect their property, and most importantly, keep their women safe from harm.

Women. They were the reason men fought and died. Sure, they said the hullaballoo had to do with slaves and property, but to his young mind it had been more about keeping the womenfolk in the way of life they were accustomed to having. Without help, southern belles would need to learn to clean their own homes and do for themselves. He didn't see that happening, not at first when his father, uncles, and brothers left. But in the end, after the men were gone and most of the help run off, too, those women learned. He'd watched it, and in his heart he didn't feel sorry for them, not one bit.

He'd been too young to go into battle according to his mama, although he tried to sneak away more than once. Fourteen should've been old enough, he argued, but she held firm. After the war, he'd stayed with her out of duty. His pa would've wanted—no, expected—as much. But the woman wasn't cut out for tending a household, and it killed her pretty quickly. And the minute after she took her last wheezing breath, he placed two pennies on her eyelids, nodded to his aunts and sister, and walked out the front door.

Clive had never looked back. He didn't plan to set foot on Georgia soil ever again, so he brushed it right off his boots, mind, and heart. Nothing left there for him. Nothing.

But now this golden-haired beauty with the emerald eyes seated across from him nearly made him forget his vow to not be taken in by a woman's wiles. A delicate shade of pink bloomed across her cheeks, giving her creamy complexion an added layer of color. He'd seen paintings in Paris that showed women, mostly wearing very little clothing, with the same kind of heightened appearance. They'd attracted him then, and this living, breathing, come-to-life beauty caught his interest now.

Her hands were clasped in her lap but weren't hidden by the folds of her skirt. He glanced down at the long, slender fingers. No wedding ring. But the fingers, well, they sent his mind into places it oughtn't go. Images of those slender digits splayed across her naked bosom sent his heart beating quicker. Then his brain pulled a dirty trick and slapped an image of that hand curled around a part of him that had no business coming to mind at this moment.

He shifted in his seat, glad that she gazed out the window and not his way.

How could a woman he hadn't even exchanged pleasantries with affect him this way? It made no sense, but here he sat with semi-erect proof that she wasn't merely any random female.

Clive cleared his throat, and when she turned his way and met his gaze, he smiled.

"I do believe my mother must be spinning in her grave right about now." He nodded when her eyebrows shot up. "That's right, she raised me to be a gentleman, and here we sit without my introducing myself. I apologize for that. I'm Clive Cooper, at your service."

Her eyebrows went higher on that pretty forehead, and for an instant he wondered if she'd reply. After the experience with the other fellow in the car, he wouldn't blame her if she felt completely done in by men on trains and wanted nothing more than to steer clear of them.

He watched as she considered her options. The green eyes went from dark and suspicious to a lighter shade, as if she'd decided he seemed trustworthy.

"My name is, ah, Priscilla Buchanan. Pleased to meet you, Mr. Cooper."

Hmm, so she didn't trust him that much after all. A stumble over the introduction? Dead giveaway for taking an assumed name. He'd done it often enough to recognize the tongue tripping over an unfamiliar phrase.

Fine by him if she wanted to maintain a cautious appearance although he did wonder why she concealed herself. He doubted she ran from the law, although one could never be sure. And if she did, it didn't matter to him. He'd hidden from local lawmen a time or two. Maybe a husband looked for her. Another peek at her ring finger shot that thought to bits. No deep groove in her soft skin to indicate she'd removed a gold band.

Must be something that made her take an alias. Not his business, though.

A tip of his chin toward his chest and what he hoped came away as a friendly expression. "The pleasure's all mine, Miss Buchanan."

****

Clive had several things that rattled his chains. Some were slight annoyances, the kind a man could dismiss with a shake of the head, but others got his blood boiling. He worked at it to keep his temper under control. Back when he'd been younger, that hotheadedness had gotten him into too many scrapes to count. Worse, it had cost him what he could never recover, more valuable than gold and much more precious.

The past could not be erased, but it did have a bearing on the present.

Once Miss Buchanan settled into the seat across from him, he waited a while. No need to startle her any with unexpected movements. And he didn't want her to get the idea he vacated his seat permanently. No, no reason to let the lady wonder if the bothersome man she'd just given the slip to might resettle in his place.

He'd learned to read people. He had to, or he'd be dead by now.

It didn't take much to see the woman seated nearby had come from a good home. The dark blue traveling ensemble she wore looked expensive, although it didn't sit tightly on her form. She'd lost weight recently, he'd put silver on it.

That she traveled alone gave him cause to wonder, but that wasn't what boiled his grits. Women living lives beyond the constraints of their family upbringing weren't as uncommon as one would imagine. He'd seen enough ladies passing through the world on their own, trying to make a life worth living to not think much of it.

But he couldn't stand men who disrespected women. Even if the world was changing and more women were in different circumstances than before the war and westward expansion, there were rules to be followed. Men had an obligation to be civilized around the fairer sex, and the fellow idly picking his teeth in the seat a few rows back had not held up his part of the practice.

When it appeared as if the woman had calmed and gazed out the window at the scenery, he stood. She looked up, but he shook his head at her questioning gaze.

"I'm just stepping out for a breath of air, is all. Be back before my seat cools, even."

She gave a gentle nod, then turned her attention back to the world passing beyond the window. They'd reached a stretch of green, lush farmland and rolling hills. Trees, branches dripping with leaves. Dandelions dotted the pastures.

Certainly a lot different from where he headed. Once he took care of this bit of business, he'd be grateful to sit and admire the view—both outside the window and seated across from him.

The car had filled a bit, so chatter, coupled with the rumble of steel wheels on the tracks, made the space noisy. He had no worry he'd be overheard, but he leaned down when he reached the man.

Slick, the kind of greasy look that reminded him of something that slid on its belly through slime at the edge of a pond. Toads and newts, the kind he remembered from childhood. The occasional garden snake, sliding along through the back acreage at his parents' rural Georgia farm. He'd never appreciated those creatures the way his older brother and younger sister had.

His younger sister. Maybe if she hadn't cottoned so much to slithery beings, she mightn't have been so trusting.

But thinking on Addie right now wouldn't do him any good. And it certainly wouldn't help her one bit, either.

Guilt over leaving her when their ma passed shot through him. If he let them, the emotions that stirred when he recalled his sister could drop him to his knees, so he pushed them aside. No time for regrets. He'd have eternity to carry that pain.

If the obnoxious fellow realized he drew near, he gave no sign.

Clive cleared his throat. Loudly.

The man picked at his teeth with a splintered toothpick. One end sprouted tiny wood hairs, as if it had been dragged across a rock instead of in a person's mouth. Now he stuck the sliver in the corner of his mouth and furrowed his brow. His gaze barely concealed his annoyance at being interrupted.

"What?" The slouch straightened. His gaze shot to a worn leather bag on the floor at his feet.

"Now I'd expect a man like you to know better than to pack his firearm in his saddlebag." Clive undid the button on his jacket and let the front fall to the side. He wore a pair of Colt revolvers on his hips, so he gave the other man a second to see he carried before he spoke again. "Why, if'n you're gonna go around annoying people, you should be sure to have some protection at your fingertips."

The glare he received could've drilled a hole in his head if he weren't immune to stares from ornery men. He'd seen enough that this one didn't intimidate him one bit.

To his credit, the other man didn't go for his bag. Smart enough to see it would only bring him pain, most likely with a hole in his belly. No, he stared, silently, just the way those pond lizards had done.

Since he didn't want to waste time, Clive got straight to the point. "Look, the whole car saw how insolent you were with that young lady." When the other opened his mouth to protest, he cut him off. "Now, don't insult me by tryin' to deny it. Facts are facts. Fact is, you behaved like an ass." He gave it a moment to sink in before his tipped his chin toward the other end of the car, where Miss Buchanan sat. "I don't believe the woman would appreciate an apology from you, or I'd march you over there to deliver it. I don't think she cares to ever hear your voice again, so I'm encouragin' you to keep your yap closed if you ever see her again."

The man's jaw dropped. He straightened and pulled his feet beneath him.

Clive waited for the other to begin to rise from the seat before he planted a hand on the man's chest and pushed. He fell back against the upholstery with a satisfying slap.

"Oof!" Brows tightened, and a finger rose in the air between them. "Now hold on! You can't treat me this way!"

He leaned so close he smelled the sour stench that floated the man's words into existence. "Oh, so you don't like being disrespected? Now you know how ladies feel when you act like a smug windbag." He waved his hand in front of his face. "A stinky one, at that. Look, stay away from that woman seated over yonder if you know what's good for you. And if I ever catch you disrespectin' a woman again…well, let's just say I won't promise not to introduce you to my two friends." He straightened and pushed his jacket back so the pistols were again in view. "The Colt sisters, well, they're even more testy when it comes to reptiles like you treating ladies with disregard."

When he walked away, he didn't look back. Snakes rarely attacked when they realized they were outdone. Besides, before the man could press the trigger on whatever he kept in his bag, Clive'd have one, maybe two, shots off. He'd hear the other's hammer being pulled back moments before the man could bring the gun up and take aim.

And Clive? He wouldn't need to aim to take the no-gooder out. Instinct, born of years of killing for hire, gave him the advantage.

****

Pansy had no idea why she'd given the man a fake name. It came without thought, fell from her lips as if her mind knew better than she did how to deal with this new situation. Because it certainly wasn't anything she'd experienced before leaving Charleston, introducing herself to strange men.

Good Lord, but Father would have a conniption fit if he could see her now.

But he can't, she reminded herself. What she said and did now had nothing to do with her parents, or anyone for that matter. Her life, her decisions.

This Mr. Cooper was easy on the eyes. Not in the fussy, carpetbaggy way that the oaf still shooting her dirty looks from his position farther down the car had. No, this man came across as rugged, right from the tips of his dusty boots to the dark brown waves that fell to his shoulders.

A tiny scar skittered across his left temple. Old and faded, but still discernable. She wondered how he'd gotten it. A childhood mishap? Or a war wound, although she didn't think him quite old enough to have served. But who could tell? Both sides had taken on boys who were far from manhood.

It didn't matter, though. She had no business considering any man's business, not even the tiniest bit of it, including a scar. No, she'd be better off if she'd keep her mind on topics that concerned her, like where to settle and what to do when she got there. Not knowing one solitary soul on the western face of God's green earth had its disadvantages. No one would welcome her arrival or offer a safe haven for her to lay her head. No, she'd have to rely on herself for everything.

Couldn't waste a minute contemplating a stranger's features, or anything else about him, for that matter. She had more pressing things to occupy her mind and time.

A list. She should make a list of all the things she needed to do when she reached her destination.

She hoped she recognized where she was meant to be when she got there.

That could not be a worry now. Not ever, really, because fretting over what can't be changed is a silly woman's game. And she, Pansy Mae Bloom, did not consider herself silly.

Her bag held all sorts of necessary items, including a gift from Daisy. A writer, the older sister had pressed the brown leather journal into Pansy's hands the day she'd gone west with Lily. If she closed her eyes, she could still hear Daisy's lilting words. She'd accompanied her sisters to the stagecoach depot. Just before they boarded for the first leg of their trip, the one pulled a package from her valise and handed it over.

"Every chapter of life deserves to be told. Remember that. You're in charge of your own destiny." Her sister pulled her in for a fast sideways hug. She smelled of ink and books with a hint of verbena thrown in. "Don't let anyone tell you otherwise, do you hear me? Write your own story, little sister. Do what makes you happy, and don't listen to anyone else. You know yourself better than anyone ever could…but don't let Mother or Father know I gave that kind of advice." She grinned, and Pansy wished she could keep her sister home with them, even if it were only for a day or two longer.

"I won't." She imagined their parents would frown on such guidance. They, of course, expected her to bow to their wishes and accept their plans for her as indisputable. She hated to see Daisy leave. Out of all her sisters, she felt closest to the daring writer among them. Despite her heart cracking as the stagecoach readied to pull away, she forced a smile onto her face. "Your advice is safe with me." A lump grew in her throat, making it hard to catch a breath. "But I promise, I will do what makes me happy."

Daisy put her arms out and gave her a big hug. She

spoke near Pansy's cheek. "And write it all down. Tell your story, sister, because I don't want you to forget any details. Someday we'll be together again, and I'll want to hear all about what you were doing when we were apart." A fast kiss on the cheek before she turned and climbed into the coach behind Lily.

The door slammed, and Daisy had leaned from the window to wave. The last she'd seen of her sister.

Now she opened her traveling satchel and reached inside. Her fingers closed around the soft leather book. She pulled it out and stared at its cover. The gift brought both joy and sadness. Would she ever see Daisy again? Had that one last wave been the end of their physical contact? For all she knew, Mother, Father, and Daisy were reunited with their lost son and brother in heaven. Maudlin thought, but it could be true.

The thoughtful parting gift still sat empty, each page as pristine as when the volume had been given. She traced a fingertip over the cover, imagining she could feel the imprint her sister left behind.

Time to begin, she thought.

Mr. Cooper cleared his throat. A deep, masculine sound that caught her attention. When she looked up, he smiled.

"A good book, Miss Buchanan?"

A small bottle of ink and pen were tucked into a length of waterproofed fabric, so she felt around for them inside her bag with one hand while she held the journal with the other. Her gaze locked on his, a smile turning her lips high in the corners when she found the necessary items.

"It will be."

If he'd been about to engage her further, she didn't

know for sure. He seemed as if he might, so she made a great show of preparing to write, opening the book, and staring off into the distance above his head. It took all her concentration to not glance down at the man, especially when she remembered his deep, brooding gaze.

She unwrapped the length of leather cord that held the book closed, opened it, and angled the pages so no one could peek. She began to write in her finest hand. Or as fine as she could manage given the swaying of the moving train.

October 15, 1879. In a Union Pacific railcar headed toward my destiny, wherever that may be…

Chapter 3

"Next stop, Chicago." The uniformed conductor made his way through the crowded railcar, raising his voice to be heard above the scrape of leather cases being removed from the overhead compartment and the chatter of excited travelers. "Chicago, next stop."

Pansy had not thought to disembark in the city, but travel weariness made her back ache. She needed to stretch, and some fresh air might chase away the pain in her head. Even with the windows open, the air inside the car reeked of sweat, onions, and body odor. She'd taken to holding a scented hanky in front of her nose, but it couldn't entirely mask the odors.

Definitely time to step off the train. A few hours of exploration and a change of scenery would do her good. She stood when the train slowed.

Since she had begun writing in her journal, the man seated across from her had gone silent. When she tucked her writing implements into her case and pulled out a copy of Melvin's *Moby Dick*, he'd looked about to comment, so she had held the book high and feigned concentration. The truth, that she had read the book twice already, did not need to be shared with him. Her business, not his.

The resolve to keep herself from anyone who might offer advice on anything she thought or did hadn't diminished. If anything, it grew with every passing mile.

This adventure, with its first taste of independence, strengthened her determination to forge her own path in life.

She stood and waited for the pins and needles prickling her toes to subside. When they did, she reached for her traveling bag. Large enough to accommodate necessities, but not so heavy that she wouldn't be able to manage on her own.

"Do you have family in Chicago?"

The man across from her stood, making the space between the seats shrink. Not a wide man, but tall and muscular, he had a presence that drew attention. She imagined he caught the eye of every female in the car the minute he got to his feet. A glance down showed the man's black boot tips were worn. The dust had mostly faded, visible now only in the deep creases in the leather.

"Miss Buchanan?"

Miss Buchanan. The unfamiliar name didn't catch her attention, but his loud tone did. She looked up when she realized he'd been talking to her.

"Pardon?" Daydreaming about a man's boots kept her from having any idea what he'd been saying. "Were you speaking to me?"

She'd noticed a lot about the man, from the way he sat with rugged ease, to the little scar on his face, to the set of his lips as he watched the miles disappear through the window on the coach wall beside their seats. But until this very moment, she hadn't taken a deep look at his eyes.

They were the color of a stormy sky. Flecks of darker gray in his irises gave them depth, and when he locked his gaze on her, a shiver ran up her spine. Fear? Excitement? Hard to tell.

A tip of his chin toward his chest. "I remarked about Chicago being your destination. Do you have family here?"

She shook her head. "No."

"Friends?"

Another shake.

"Well, are you staying with someone you trust?" His brow furrowed. A tilt of his head dropped a lock of hair over one eye, but he swiped it back. "Not trying to be nosey, ma'am. It's just that Chicago is a big city and you're…"

She fisted her free hand on her hip. Exactly what she intended to escape, people telling her who she was, what she thought, and how she should behave. Why, she'd intentionally avoided giving this man an opportunity to get to know her, yet he clearly thought he had the right to comment on her life.

"I'm what?"

If Mother were alive, she'd have something to say about the brash tone she took with him, privately of course, but no one remained to dictate how Pansy should act. If her mother looked down from the hereafter with horror, then so be it.

The man lifted one eyebrow but didn't instantly reply. His gaze remained neutral despite the combative tone she'd taken.

"You're a woman who obviously doesn't need a stranger's advice. Pardon me, Miss Buchanan, if I've overstepped." He tipped his chin toward his chest and offered a reconciliatory smile.

But it wasn't his lips that held her attention. No, the man's eyes pulled her in. Had she not been so determined to not let another person tell her what to do or influence her actions, she might have fallen into their depths. They looked so safe.

She chided herself for giving in to his handsomeness—and her personal vulnerability. If she were to make it on her own, she'd have to toughen up. A lot.

"You're right about that, sir. I can do just fine without uninvited suggestions." She nodded toward the aisle. He stood too close for her to pass without brushing against his body. "If you'll step aside, please."

****

Minutes before the train pulled into the Chicago station, she made a snap decision to disembark. Her back hurt from sitting, and the man across from her had been trying to catch her eye for a while. She'd avoided meeting his gaze and giving him the opening to begin a conversation, but the effort wore on her. Better to take a walk in the sunshine.

But the sun hid behind heavy gray clouds, and even though she'd stored her trunk at the depot, the bag she carried felt heavier with each step she took. And those were a challenge, too. She'd grown up walking the cobbled lanes of Charleston. These bumpy, rutted walkways were a far cry from those smooth paths.

And Chicago didn't impress Pansy the way she'd hoped it might. In her musings she'd thought the city to be filled with tall buildings and lit up with the new electrical lightbulbs she'd heard so much about. Some of that held true, but not to the extent she'd hoped.

What she saw would have been best viewed from behind the window of the train car.

Dusty, grimy streets. Many new buildings, built after the big fire of eighteen seventy-one, stood in sharp contrast to the older edifices, but still the place didn't impress. It lacked the charm she'd hoped to see.

Well, no help for that.

And loud. The city teemed with carts, pedestrian traffic, and riders. A bus rolled past, sending a fresh cloud of dust into the air. She brought her elbow high and buried her face in the crook of her arm, but not before she'd inhaled a lungful of grit.

The coughing fit that came upon her made her double over for a moment. Her throat stung, and her eyes ran. Standing on a Chicago street corner hacking her brains out had not been on her must-do list, and the experience made her wish she'd stayed on the train.

She didn't see the man who brushed against her but felt his hand on her wrist an instant before he tugged the ribbons holding her reticule in place.

"St—" A fresh wave stole her breath.

She turned in time to see the figure dash through the crowd, her bag dangling from one fist. A fast look around didn't show any law nearby to help, so she hitched up her skirt and took a few steps before another cough forced her to stop.

A second figure ran past her. She couldn't tell who it was. Police, perhaps?

"Here, take a drink." A woman appeared beside her holding a chipped white coffee mug in her hand. "Water will help."

Thank goodness for some mercy, Pansy thought as she downed the liquid. Tepid, but it washed away the tickle and scratch left by the dust she'd inhaled. When the cup was empty, she handed it back.

"Thank you."

The woman nodded, her tired blue eyes

compassionate. A tendril of hair escaped its bun and brushed the shoulder of faded brown dress she wore, making a wispy brown spiral on the slender frame. "I saw what happened." She tilted her head toward the coffee shop behind them as she wiped a workworn hand down the front of her dress. The shop sat on the corner, at the intersection of two rough-looking streets. "Not uncommon in this neighborhood. What is a fine lady like yourself doin' on this side of the tracks?"

It hit Pansy then that not only were the streets filthy, but the buildings were shabby, too. Run-down, a series of boarded-up windows across the one next to the coffee shop.

"I guess I made a wrong turn." She looked back, toward the train depot, and wished she'd stayed safely on the train.

"Well, where are you headed? I can give you some direction, if you've got yourself turned around."

The other's kindness touched her heart so deeply that the backs of her eyes tingled. Where was she headed? A good question, but she could hardly begin that discussion with a perfect stranger.

She sucked in a shaky breath and tried to pull a smile onto her face. "I'm not headed anywhere in particular." She shrugged, shifting her bag from her left hand to her right. "I wanted to see a bit of Chicago, so I got off the train and thought I'd walk around for a while before I catch the next train west."

The woman couldn't be much older than she was, but the weary shake of her head, dip to her thin shoulders, and fine lines etched in her face showed she had lived a harder life. She gave a tired sigh. "Well, that didn't work out well, now did it?" A thumb jerked toward the coffee shop. "Come on in, sit a while, and get somethin' in your belly. The world will still be a hard place sometimes, but at least you'll be full."

Her reticule. It had the money she'd allotted for her trip. And now it was who knew where with that awful man who'd robbed her.

When she hesitated, the other woman threaded her free hand through Pansy's arm and tugged her toward the shop's open doorway. "It's okay. I'll make you a sandwich and a cup of coffee. No charge." She offered a small smile. "We can't let you go on your way thinkin' all folks in Chicago are horrid, now can we?"

On her way. Her train ticket, in her reticule, with the thief.

Grateful to the woman for giving her a chance to sit and ponder for a bit, she sighed. "That's very kind of you."

The kindness of strangers. Mother had always said it came at the right time and blessed those who need it most.

****

Clive could have let the thief run off without giving chase. It would have been easier, but he'd never been one for taking the simplest way out of a fix. Even though he hardly knew the woman whose property he went after— hell, he didn't know her at all—it didn't sit well with him to witness a crime and not attempt to do the right thing.

The man who tore the reticule from the young woman's wrist ran faster than a starving hound after a rabbit. He knew the city's series of alleyways well enough to dash in and out of them without stopping to consider whether to zigzag right or left. At every turn, the distance between them grew.

Trash littered the ground, turning the packed dirt lanes treacherous. He avoided stepping in rotting fruits and vegetables. Missed falling over a heap of half-burned, busted lumber. Sidestepped a skeletal dog. Whether living or dead, he couldn't tell but knew better than to run into it.

He pulled in a deep breath. Between his vest, jacket, gun belt, and hat, he carried so much extra weight it began to slow him down. A stitch tore through his right side. Not so bad that he stopped, but enough of a stab that it caught his attention.

Time to give it all he had left and grab the sonofabitch.

The man took a fast right, dashing into a tight alleyway ahead, and Clive did the same.

And that, blindly following a known criminal into a small dark space was a mistake. The instant he turned the corner, Clive's head collided with something hard enough to send him flying backward. He landed on a pile of greasy papers that were flattened against the wooden back wall of a building. His stomach rebelled at the stench of rancid fat, but he didn't heave.

A hand to his right temple where a knot already formed. His fingers came away dry, so the bastard hadn't cut his head wide open.

"Sonofabitch!" Nothing he hated more than letting someone get the best of him, and that had certainly just happened. Years of training, hours in the field avoiding detection while tracking others, and he'd fallen prey to a stupid mistake. He'd let his mind wander and his emotions best him, had given the other man the opportunity to strike out.

Well, there was little to do now. He'd lost the thief

down the alley. From where he sat, he saw nothing but garbage between the two buildings that formed the tight lane and a wooden fence at the far side.

No sign of man or mouse. Rat, probably, but even they were hidden from his sight although it occurred to him he should get up before something hungry considered him food. He stood and wiped a hand over the back of his blue jean trousers. The fabric, softened with age and washing, survived the ordeal. Nothing unsavory came off on his palm, so he headed for the alley.

Tighter and smellier than he expected, the space hardly offered enough room for a man to walk without turning to one side. A miracle that the other had enough room to swing that slab of wood at him the way he had. When he reached the fence, he stepped onto an overturned barrel and hoisted himself up so he could look over. On the other side, another debris-littered alley. Just as narrow and putrid smelling as this one.

As he turned to jump down, he spotted the item that had led him on this chase, so he hitched a leg over the top of the fence. Might as well get something for his trouble. On the other side, he grabbed the reticule from the dirt and tucked it into his jacket pocket. Then he scaled the fence a second time and headed back, hoping he remembered how to get out of the maze of alleyways.

****

The coffee shop wasn't fancy. Four battered tables surrounded by an assortment of rickety chairs filled the humble space. What it lacked in character and décor, it made up for in cleanliness and fare.

Pansy's gaze wandered over the wide wooden floorboards. They were swept clean enough that she felt confident she could have sat on them without worrying she'd soil her skirt. The air, scented with cinnamon and coffee, made her mouth water the instant she walked into the place.

She'd taken a table near the front glass window. A place to look out onto the passersby who moved quickly and with purpose. They had places to go and were used to being part of this grimy world. Unlike her, who had stumbled onto a seedy part of town without even considering the characters of those who populated it. What a fool she'd been.

Well, lesson learned. Time to stop bumbling through life. If she planned to take control of her future, which she most definitely did, she'd have to be more prudent about what she did in the present.

Leah, the woman who came to her assistance, came from a back room with a plate in one hand and a mug of coffee in the other. She placed both on the table in front of Pansy, then stepped back. "Can I get you anything else?"

A shake of her head. It humbled her that she could not pay for the meal. The reticule held her spending money. Sure, she had sewn silver into the hem and seams of her skirt and jacket, but she couldn't very well begin taking her clothing apart here.

"No, thanks. I appreciate the meal." She looked down at the plate. Two slices of thick bread beneath a slab of turkey covered in gravy. A tidy heap of peas. A generous serving of mashed potatoes. The aromas were intoxicating. "You shouldn't have gone to so much trouble. Everything looks delicious, thank you."

A nod, then a sweep of a hand toward the meal. "You're welcome. Now, eat before everythin' goes cold.

And holler if you need more coffee."

"I will, thanks." When the woman turned and walked away, Pansy picked up the fork that had arrived on the side of the plate and looked around for a knife. There wasn't one, so she pressed the side of her fork into the turkey and cut it that way.

Holler if you need more coffee. She hadn't yet reached the west, yet so much was different from what she'd grown accustomed to. No white napkins or full sets of utensils and the uncovered table made her wish for one of Mother's white linen cloths.

But those were gone now, all the finery of their home in Charleston. Lost to time and circumstance, sold to pay for funerals and this westward adventure. She couldn't look back, not yet, anyway. It tore at her too much to remember all that she'd given up. All that had been taken from her.

Time to eat, so she began. The food smelled fantastic, but she hardly tasted it. There could have been old socks on her plate, and she mightn't have known the difference. Memories of what she'd had, and thoughts of what she'd never know again, filled her mind.

Her heart cracked, thinking of that life. The ache in her chest came upon her so strongly that she placed the fork on the edge of her plate and put a hand over the center of her chest. She closed her eyes and focused on breathing. A lump had formed in her throat, making even that small task difficult. How to breathe when a death grip wrapped around her neck?

"Are you okay?"

That voice. A shiver shot up her spine.

Must be the excitement.

She opened her eyes and peered up into the face of

the man from the train. Clive Cooper. She'd thought never to see him again, yet here he stood. His gaze held hers, and she saw warmth and kindness in his stare.

"Miss Buchanan? Are you okay?" He pulled his brows together and peered intently into her eyes. "You've gone pale. Are you feeling poorly?"

A second shiver sent her nerve endings tingling. Nope, it wasn't the excitement that set her senses swirling, unless she counted the exhilaration of seeing his chiseled features so near her face. He'd leaned down and peered into her eyes as if he expected to unlock one of the mysteries of civilization in their depths.

It would be easy to lean forward…

Get hold of yourself!

She shook her head, dropped her hands from where they still rested between her breasts, and straightened her spine against the hard wooden chair. Was she feeling poorly? One way to put it, she supposed, but not in the way he probably imagined.

"No, I'm okay." She remembered her manners. Mother might be gone from this earth, but she'd never be far from her daughter's heart. All the lessons on etiquette weren't wasted. "Thank you for your concern, but I'm fine."

As fine as she could be considering the circumstances. But she didn't elaborate.

The man straightened up when she reassured him, although his forehead between his eyes held a deep crease. Disbelief, she supposed as she kept an outwardly calm demeanor. She wondered how he'd react if she reached up and stuck a piece of silver into the channel his skepticism carved into his face. Surely the silver would stick right into the crevasse, held tight by his expression.

If she had silver to spare, she just might do it, but, of course, she currently found herself in financial straits. Not entirely, but she had no intention of disassembling her clothing to find change—especially not for the purpose of jamming it into a man's forehead!

"Well, I'm glad to hear that. You've been through a lot today, and I'd hate to see you take a bad turn." He'd removed his hat and held it loosely in his hand. Even bareheaded, the man looked large in the confined space. Suddenly the whitewashed walls felt closer than they had been and the furnishings smaller. "Wouldn't do one bit."

Her turn to show incredulity. She raised one eyebrow and concentrated on counting to ten, as Mother had taught her to do before speaking her mind. A bad habit she had always had, opening her mouth and letting thoughts tumble out without considering their effect.

"I've been through 'a lot'? Is that what you'd call being accosted by a slug in a suit on a train, then having a wolf steal my possessions?" Her voice rose with each word, but she couldn't help herself. Not even counting could save her from spilling her thoughts. "Men! Everywhere, ruining a woman's life with their animalistic ways. Why, a woman can barely get a bite to eat without a man showing up to ask if she might fall onto her knees and beg his assistance. Or, better yet, drop over from the sheer 'a lot'ness of her day!"

Mr. Cooper had the good sense to take a step back. She couldn't blame him, not one bit. She must look crazy to the man, and she knew it, but the dam had opened, and there wasn't any way to stem the flood.

"I didn't mean anything impertinent, Miss Buchanan." He twirled his hat in his hand by its brim. A nervous affliction? Maybe. Or perhaps he stood contemplating how quickly he could run in the face of her fury. She couldn't tell. "I only worried for your welfare, that's it. I didn't intend to be an animal stalking you at your dinner, I assure you."

His earnest stare quenched the fire that sent her emotions bubbling over. Some, but not all. As he waited for her reply, Pansy picked up the fork resting on the edge of her nearly empty plate. She didn't remember eating all the food, but now she speared the last bit of turkey. She brought it to her mouth and shoved it in. Their gazes locked as she chewed and swallowed. Then, she ate the rest of the mashed potatoes. Barely a mouthful, but it gave her a moment to consider what she'd say next.

Already Mother's voice rang in her head. *Pansy, you're being impetuous again. That's no way for a well-bred southern young lady to behave.*

Well, with no one to help her navigate the rest of her life, she decided not to feel guilt from the grave. If Mother wanted to dictate what her daughter should say and do, she should've stuck around instead of being a voice inside her mind.

Instant remorse chilled Pansy's hot head. Mother had tried to stay. So hard, she'd struggled to remain, so giving her a mental sassing was unfair. Not kind, either, to clamp down so disrespectfully on the man who had done nothing but help her since they met.

She swallowed. Then, looked away. Leah leaned in the doorway to the kitchen. Must be they'd made enough noise to grab her attention. A smile, to let the kind woman know nothing bad happened in her coffee shop. She acknowledged the gesture before heading back to her stove.

She placed the fork on the empty plate. Smoothed a hand over her hair. Swallowed around the tightness in her throat.

It took some effort to meet the man's gaze, but she managed. Barely.

"I'm sorry. It's no excuse, but you're right. Today has been…" She searched for a word that would cover the enormity of a distressing day that wasn't even nearly over.

"A lot." His tone held no anger, nor did his eyes. Kindness shone down on her. "More than most wom—ah, folks would care to endure on any given day. Just, a lot."

The fact that he kept himself from attributing her outburst to her being female made the stranger endearing. And even with their time together on the train, he remained a stranger, despite the fact every time he spoke her heart skipped a beat.

"Thank you. I don't generally act so childishly." She lifted her shoulders, then let them fall. Weariness swept over her, and the act of explaining wore her out. "I've never been in a position to accept a charity meal, and while I'm grateful, it's still difficult to cope. I don't know what I'll do without my reticule. My funds, ticket, portrait of my—"

It hit her like a ton of bricks. The small velvet-cased portrait of her parents. She'd kept it close, in her reticule. And now it was lost.

"Intended?"

The word he supplied would have made her laugh had she not been so heartbroken. It was the only likeness she had of them, and now she would never see it again.

A tear slid from one eye, sliding hot and wet down her cheek.

Mr. Cooper's eyes widened. "Forgive me, I'm sorry—I didn't mean to make you cry. It's not my business whose portrait you carry. Your husband, intended, child...none of it needs explaining to me." He reached for his back pocket and pulled out the same bandana she'd seen him wipe across his brow on the train. She took it and dabbed her eyes with it. "I apologize. I spoke without thinking."

She took a moment to collect herself. Then, she wiped the fabric over her cheeks before meeting his gaze. It pained her that she'd distressed him. The handsome, rugged fellow looked entirely unsettled by her display of emotion.

"You've got nothing to apologize for. It's me who should be asking forgiveness." She held the bandana out, but he waved it off, so she dropped her hand to her lap. "The portrait in my reticule is my parents. Or was them. No, they still are my parents but...they've passed on. The little likeness is the only one I have of them, and now it's gone." The backs of her eyes prickled again, but before a tear fell, the man reached into his jacket pocket and pulled out her reticule and handed it to her.

"I chased the man who took it. I didn't catch him, but he threw your property on the ground. That's why I came looking for you." He tapped his leg with his Stetson and nodded to the bag. "I hope your parents' portrait is still in there. I could be wrong, but when I tucked it in my pocket, I thought it felt like something remained inside."

Pansy jiggled it. Surely, he wasn't mistaken. A slash of dirt covered one corner, and one of the ribbons that held it on her wrist had torn, but there were contents inside. She tugged at the remaining ribbon, and when it gave way, she turned the bag out on the table.

The small burgundy purse her sister Lily had given her for her fourteenth birthday was missing. It held her funds, so she still sat destitute. But the velvet portrait holder remained. She opened it, and her heart rose. Her parents' faces stared back at her.

"My parents." She held the portrait out. They had dressed for the sitting and looked well turned out, if somewhat somber. What she wouldn't give to see them smile again. She closed the album with a gentle snap and held it to her breast. "Thank you for your trouble. This means the world to me. Truly, it does."

A slow grin crept across the man's face. "Happy to help, although it doesn't look like your money is here. I imagine it would be in a purse, but I don't see one."

Very observant. No purse, but a few hairpins and her train ticket spread across the tabletop.

"No purse, unfortunately. And aside from the money that's gone, the purse itself had sentimental value." She pushed the hairpins into a pile and picked up the ticket. "At least this is here, or I'd be stranded in Chicago."

She gathered the pins and slipped them back into her reticule. Then, the portrait of her parents. Until it was washed and the ribbons replaced, the item held little usefulness, so she opened her bigger bag and dropped it inside. The train ticket fit into a jacket pocket.

"You don't plan to stay in Chicago, then?"

"No, I don't." It sounded foolish considering what happened, but she went on. "I just wanted to get some air. Maybe see the city, especially the water tower. I heard that it's one of the only buildings that survived the fire a few years back. It's taller than any building I've seen, and it must be strong to still be standing." She lifted her shoulders, then let them drop. Such a silly idea, to walk out into a strange city hoping to look at, of all things, a water tower. If she wasn't so worn out from the day, she'd be embarrassed. "I didn't see it, and now I'm going back to the train depot before I meet any more unsavory Chicago characters."

Pansy stood and grabbed her bag from the chair beside hers, then went over to thank Leah. The woman had returned to her spot in the doorway between the kitchen and front room, and straightened when she went over to her.

"I'm grateful for your kindness. The meal was one of the best I've ever had." She reached an arm out and gave the other woman a fast hug. Scents of garlic and peppers swept up her nose, and she imagined there would be something tasty on tonight's menu. "I'm sorry I can't compensate you for the food."

The other woman shook her head. "Not necessary. I'm sorry you got such a bad impression of our city." She glanced at the man walking toward the open front door. "I hope the rest of your travels will be much smoother."

"Thank you. I do, too."

Pansy turned for the exit. As she passed the table she'd occupied, she spied a silver coin beside her empty plate. Only one person could have placed it there, and he waited for her beside the door.

Chapter 4

Clive looked over at the sleeping woman. Whatever her name, she presented a lovely sight. Face relaxed, as if she hadn't lost some of her belongings to a thief. Long, dark eyelashes lay across her cheeks. Occasionally they fluttered, and the movement intrigued him.

The train out of Chicago wasn't as full as the one they'd traveled on earlier, and they had been able to secure seats in a quieter car. When he'd accompanied her to the depot, then followed her into the car, she hadn't objected to his presence. The seats they took were at the front of the carriage. He'd settled into the one that placed his back against the wall, facing into the passengers and potential trouble. She hadn't objected to that, either.

They hadn't spoken much before she fell asleep, which was fine by him. The less attached he became to her, the better. Soon he'd exit the train, she'd leave his acquaintance, and he could get back to living the life he knew best. Loner, sometimes gunslinger, and most importantly, man unencumbered by romance.

But now, while this pretty, yet mysterious, woman rested? He'd drink his fill of her sweet beauty, carve her face into his mind so he would remember her always.

Clive couldn't explain it, but the woman, whatever her real name was, had touched a part of him he'd thought long dead. And she had done it without any of the maneuvering women favored when dealing with men. Long ago, he had tired of those transparent attempts to pull him into a romantic situation. He would not be a slave to his heart—or another's, for that matter.

When he needed carnal release, there were women who made their livelihood providing that service. He never minded paying for a warm body to lie with him without expectations he'd fall in love with her.

Leave that to others.

But it did no harm to gaze upon a beautiful woman, so he tilted his hat forward so the brim shaded his eyes and watched the so-called Miss Buchanan slumber. Soon enough, they'd part ways. Until then, he would do something he didn't ordinarily do. He'd indulge.

****

After they left Chicago, the train seemed to pick up speed. Surely, the notion came as a result of her imagination, but Pansy enjoyed the way there were fewer, then no, signs of civilization as they journeyed westward.

The view outside the train window changed.

Here and there, a homestead in the distance. Miles of fencing, some of it tilted and appearing as if it couldn't contain a pet duck while others were tall and sturdy looking. She wondered about the men who erected those fences. What did they hope to keep in? Maybe more importantly, what were they attempting to keep out?

The letters in her case called to her. They were tangible evidence that she wasn't completely alone in the world, a comfort against the feeling that she belonged nowhere, to no one. The bag beside her opened easily, and she reached in to grab a letter from the bundle. One from the middle, where the ribbon had loosened a tad and made slipping the envelope out effortless.

A glance at the envelope. Funny how three sisters could each have such distinct penmanship. She unfolded the sheet of paper and put the envelope on the seat beside her.

The writing, so small and cramped, covered the page on both sides. An army of ink ants marching in close formation to deliver news Lily thought worthy of sharing. The strict determination to not use a second sheet of paper motivated her to create these tidy lines. So often one or the other of them had urged her to write more comfortably and splurge on another sheet, but their eldest sister steadfastly refused. Set in her ways, from an early age, and no one could sway her when she put her mind to something.

September 15, 1879

Dear little Pansy,

I do hope you are keeping well. And looking out for our parents, as well. You know they are not getting any younger, and as the only daughter residing in the family home, it falls to you to keep an eye on them. I realize this is a lot to ask of someone your age, but there is no help for it. Do the best you can, and if you're ever in a quandary, just ask yourself what would I do? I, meaning me, your sister Lily. How would I handle a situation? Consider that, then let it be your guide.

Well, I suppose Mother has relayed my news already, but being your eldest sister, I feel I should tell you myself, as well. I have gotten married to a good, kind man named Theodore Harvey. I met Theo right when I stepped off the stagecoach, and we hit it off so well that we have recently tied the knot.

Theo is a homesteader, and his place is immaculate. A lovely home, built with care. Land that stretches as far as the eye can see. It snugs up on a mountain range, which gives an added sense of security. It is quiet out here, but Theo and I go to town a fair bit. He's promised I won't be separated from Daisy and Violet, and I believe him. The man is true to his word.

Living in Wylder with the others did a lot for me. You wouldn't think that, being the eldest and all, I had any maturing to do, but I did. And being with our sisters in Violet's little lavender house taught me more than I thought I needed to learn.

So remember that, sister. No matter how much you think you know, you don't know everything. There is still room to grow—even for me, your wise sister.

In my last letter I promised to tell you more about what we do to keep entertained out here in the west. Yes, I know it's called the wild west, but it's not as wild as you might think. Theo and I spend the evenings reading, either aloud or on our own. We both work hard during the day. He tends the property, and I tend the house, the way married couples do back home in Charleston. Instead of going to a law office the way Father does, Theo rides his horse and takes care of whatever needs attention. And instead of doing charitable work in the city the way Mother does, I do my best to keep hearth and home in order.

So, the same as in the south but a bit different, too.

But our evenings are quiet, and we are happy. I never thought to be this content, but I truly am. Again, there is no way to know everything, and this newly found joy came as a welcome surprise.

Well, I see I'm nearly out of room on this sheet of paper, so I will sign off here.

Take good care of yourself. Listen to our parents.

They know what's best, little Pansy.

And if you need more guidance, write to me and I shall do my best to tell you what to think or how to behave. I am still your eldest sister!

Much love,

Lily Harvey

What to think, indeed!

Never again, sister. I'll think for myself from here on out.

She had no knowledge of the west other than what little she'd gleaned from her sisters' letters. And those, she suspected, were full of omissions so as not to alarm her parents.

She'd read newspaper reports, but those, too, must not tell the whole truth. She couldn't imagine western towns being as barbaric as some of the stories portrayed. Goodness, how on earth could anyone live in such circumstances? Bullets filling the air, women of ill repute on every streetcorner, stampedes leveling entire towns…it didn't make sense to her that any place could be so violent.

She suspected that just as her sisters fibbed about how safe and serene the Wyoming territory could be, news reports exaggerated its rawness. They needed to sell papers while her siblings wanted to keep parental fears at bay. Two sides of the same coin. She wondered which came closer to the truth.

Well, she'd know soon enough. Union Pacific could be proud of itself. The train chugged steadily along without any interruption in service. Nice, quiet, smooth traveling. So steady, she'd taken to writing in the brown leather journal. By the time she reached a destination, she might need to invest in a second volume.

The doors to her creative ease had opened for the first time ever, and there didn't seem any way to stem the tide. Not that she wanted to. This freedom of expression relieved her soul of some of the weight she'd carried for so long. Writing her thoughts and feelings on paper gave her a way to set so much down. And when she closed the cover on both book and ink bottle, she walked away from what she'd written. No revisiting or revising, just a means to calm her mind.

She supposed that her writing process did not mimic Daisy's much, if at all. The older sister had been born a natural storyteller and had entertained them all for as long as anyone could remember. When her stories began to find their way from her mind to the paper, the family marveled at her ability, but like the others, Pansy never thought much about how it felt to put ink behind the words in a mind—until now.

Daisy had given her a gift like none she'd received before.

Now Pansy reached into her bag, returned the letter, and pulled out the journal, ink, and pen. She balanced the glass bottle on the seat beside her, dipped her pen, and composed her thoughts. Then, she began to write.

October 21, 1879

Still riding the train headed out west. It seems strange to be traveling in such comfort, when I know my sisters traveled mainly by stagecoach. And that, even with its overnight stops for lodging, had to be much more uncomfortable than this. I enjoy a pull-down berth for the night and sit in relative comfort during the daylight hours. What more could a woman want?

A plan, that's what. Now that I have finally gotten to the point in my life where I'm determined to make my

*own decisions, it is embarrassing to admit, even to the
secrecy of this journal, that I have no idea what I shall
do with my foreseeable future, let alone the rest of my
life. The uncertainty weighs heavy on me.*

*Of one thing I am certain, however. The man I met
on the first train, who also travels westward on this
second train, is kind. And handsome. He's seated across
from me right now, and I admit, I can barely keep from
staring. I never thought to be affected by a man this way,
but he's uncovered feelings in me I did not know exist.*

****

Clive didn't care much for the berth he'd claimed.
He'd never been one for confined spaces, and with the
top of the compartment scant inches from his nose, he
imagined a casket would be roomier.

He'd taken to joining in on the middle-of-the-night
poker games that took place in a smoking car. Dark and
stinking of body odor, the car didn't welcome women.
Not that any had tried to enter, but it offered a space
where men didn't need to watch their cussing or temper
their behavior. Not that they did a lot of that, anyhow,
but still, the car served as a men's-only refuge.

He hadn't taken to drinking to excess, the way some
of the others had. And he didn't play all night, as many
did. Most importantly, Clive never gambled more than
he felt comfortable losing. Not that he lost. When he did,
it was done early in a game and with the intention of
giving his fellow gamblers a sense of security.

Every night he'd been on an overnight train or boat
ride—and there many of them—he spent a few hours at
a poker table. And every one of them, he'd walked away
with heavier pockets.

He was close to calling it a night. The man in the

seat beside him stunk to high heaven, and not even the whiskey glass Clive held beneath his nose could keep the stench at bay. A fast swallow as he watched the others play out their hands.

Across from him, a loudmouth from somewhere back north set his cards on the table. A grin as he said, "I got myself a full house this time 'round. Three old ladies and a pair of sixes." He nodded toward the coins in the center. "Think I'll be takin' that pot this hand."

The man beside him folded, uttering a mild oath as he did.

Beside Clive, the smelly man snickered. "Not so fast. That pot won't be goin' anywhere with you." He slammed his cards on the table in front of him. "Four of a kind. That money's mine, I tell ya."

Clive was the only one still holding cards. He watched the man beside him reach out to rake the money in before he spoke. "Not a good idea to go touchin' another man's money." The greasy hands stopped mid-stretch. When he had everyone's attention, he laid his hand down, the five hearts lined up so sweetly against the scarred wooden backdrop. "Four through eight, and that's one pretty lookin' straight flush."

The other man pulled his hands back.

He reached for his winnings as the other players muttered about their losses and his new gain. When he had the cash in hand, he pushed his chair back and tipped his chin.

"Time to get some shut-eye."

A handful of men stood near the walls, waiting for a spot to open up at a table, so his seat didn't stay empty. Good thing, too. It saved him from having to refuse to stay in a game long after it'd lost its appeal. After days on the rails, no one smelled like roses, but he could not abide a reek that bad coming off a human.

He walked out of the end door and stood on the platform between train cars. The night air cooled his face and swept some of the stench of the railcar from his head. He tilted his head back and looked up at the sky.

When he'd been a child, his grandfather would take him out riding on the farm back in Georgia. Often, they'd camp by a stream. Those nights, they'd lie on their backs and stare up at the stars. He learned to wait patiently for shooting stars. To look closely at constellations. And perhaps most importantly, his grandfather and those star-filled skies taught him that beauty can be simple and pristine—and it can touch a man's heart more profoundly than man-made diversions.

He missed his granddad but carried his teachings along with him. They traveled way beyond the family farm, where some of his kin still lived, and lived long after the old man had taken his final breath.

A few hours till sunup. Time to catch a few winks, if he could, in the confining berth. It had been a long day. Hopefully his mind would turn off and rest would come.

Clive slid open the door to the next car. Some slept upright on hard wooden benches. Their tickets came cheaply, but they paid for the trip with discomfort. He avoided meeting anyone's gaze and walked through.

The next car was more of the same, so he kept moving.

When he finally made the first sleeper car at the end of the train, he kept going. His berth was not here. The only sign any occupied these compartments came by the sound of snores from behind closed curtains.

He expected to find the next car, which held his

bunk, quiet. But when he stepped from the car's end platform into the space itself, he saw he wasn't the only one standing. A figure stood at the far end of the carriage, one boot on the edge of the bottom berth and his hands on the edge of the top one. Clive had caught the man about to lever himself up into the bunk.

It hit him that unless Miss Buchanan had switched spots, the man attempted to climb in where she lay sleeping.

He charged forward, taking the distance from one end of the railway car to the other in a heartbeat. When he reached the other, he grabbed a handful of the fellow's jacket and pulled him backward. One foot had already been off the ground, so the man thudded to the floor, a tangle of limbs in the darkness and a series of thuds as various parts of his body bounced off the partitions on either side of the narrow aisle.

"Sonofabitch!"

Hands pushed aside curtains, and faces peered out. The thumping had alerted the sleepers, but the man's angry voice reverberated off the walls.

A stifled scream came from the berth that the man had been trying to climb into. The curtains flew back, and a familiar female face peered out. He didn't have to look long to see it was exactly who he expected.

He had more pressing matters on his hands.

The man pushed to his feet, turned, and threw a wide punch aimed at Clive's head. He'd figured the guy would lead with one, so he ducked, then swung from below. An uppercut to the bottom of a jaw, tempered to set the man back but not break anything. A fellow had to have some restraint, after all. And since he'd caught the trespasser before he could do Miss Buchanan any harm, he couldn't justify pulverizing his jaw or divesting him of his teeth.

"Why, you sonofabitch!" What he lacked in vocabulary the man made up for in brute strength. He put his head down and rushed down the aisle like an enraged bull. The confined space offered no room to sidestep, so he caught Clive right in the gut.

"Oof!" The air left his lungs in a rush. Grateful he didn't have anything in his belly to lose, he wrapped an arm around the other's neck and squeezed. He took a fast step sideways and banged the fellow's head against one of the uprights that supported the top berth beside them. "You bastard! Climbing in with women you don't know!"

His opponent grabbed one of Clive's thighs and attempted to take him to the floor, but he lifted a knee and connected with the other's nose. A crunching sound brought a howl of pain.

An explosion rang out in the railroad car, so loud it brought screams from the women cowering in their berths and hollers from the men beside them. The acrid bite of gunpowder filled the air, and smoke made the darkness murkier.

"Stop it!" He looked up to the berth that the man he wrestled had tried to enter. Miss Buchanan sat on the edge of the space, her legs dangling in midair and a pistol pointed toward the ceiling. Her finger rested on the trigger, and he had no doubt she wouldn't hesitate to press it a second time.

She tipped the business end of the weapon down and shook it at the man who'd fallen to the floor when the shot rang out. "Get up."

Clive took a step back.

Every rider in the car had gone silent. Now they

stared at the woman wearing a white nightdress, their eyes round and their mouths clamped shut.

The man held his hands in the air. "Don't shoot me. Please, don't shoot." His voice, a slurred whine as he begged for his life.

"I said get up!" She waved the gun again. In the darkness, the whites of her eyes nearly shimmered. "Now!"

"Gettin' up, I'm gettin' up!" He scrambled to his feet. His voice shook, and Clive imagined the man's testicles were trying to climb back into his belly. He almost felt sorry for him. Almost. "Don't shoot, miss. Please, I beg ya—"

The young woman leveled the gun at the man's chest. Her words were tight and low. "What the hell were you doing trying to climb up here with me?"

"I…ah…"

"I asked you a question!" She poked the gun toward him.

The man turned his head, as if looking for an escape, but Clive stood between him and the door. And on the other end, Miss Buchanan and her pistol blocked his exit.

"I was just hopin' to have some fun with ya, is all. I took notice of ya in the other car, and I, ah…"

A good thing she had a gun trained on the man, because it kept Clive from wrapping his hands around the creep's throat. How any man could think it his right to come upon an innocent woman that way was beyond him. It made him sick, just thinking about what could have happened had he not walked in at the right moment.

The bastard could've assaulted any of the women in the car. He could have begun with Miss Buchanan and worked his way through until he took advantage of all the single sleeping ladies.

Clive's fingers fisted. It took every ounce of self-control he possessed not to strangle the man.

"You're disgusting." She waved the pistol toward the door. "Get out before I have some fun of my own. I never say no to a little target practice."

The man didn't even stop to pick up his hat from where it lay in the aisle. He turned and tried to shove past Clive, but he didn't get far.

He couldn't let him just run off, so he grabbed the scoundrel by the shoulder and pushed him toward the door. When they reached the door, he slammed it open, then shoved the man out onto the platform. For an instant, he considered tossing him over the railing. No one would know, and a piece of shit would never have the chance to do wrong by a woman again.

But he couldn't do it. Not when the fellow shook so hard he could hardly stand.

He leaned so close his nose nearly touched the other's. "You bastard. If I ever see you near that woman again, I will send you to the undertaker. That's not a threat, but a promise." He shook him so hard the man's feet left the platform. "Do you understand?"

A head shake, so fast and hard the other's chin hit his own chest.

Clive released him. He pointed toward the cars behind them. "Get the hell out of here before I change my mind and throw you off. And you'd best be getting off at the next stop if you know what's good for you."

When he had seen the man walk through the next car and out onto its platform, he turned and went back inside the sleeper car. Most of the other travelers had drawn their curtains. At least one already snored. But the woman in the top berth who'd nearly been assaulted? Well, she was far from sleep.

Miss Buchanan, or whatever her name was, sat with her legs dangling over the edge of her bunk. She'd placed the pistol down, but as he crossed the space, he saw it wasn't far. At her right hand, beside her hip, where it wouldn't take more than a second to pick it up and point the business end toward any new threat.

He didn't blame her one bit for feeling a need to guard herself that way. In her position, he'd be doing the same.

Clive stood a few feet from her, close enough to whisper and be heard but not so near he'd look like a threat.

"Would you like to step out onto the platform and get some fresh air?" He knew it wasn't seemly for a woman to go out in her nightdress with a man who wasn't her husband, but she could probably use the break from the confines of the dark car. "The stars are especially bright tonight, and the air is sweet. A good way to clear the head, I think."

She didn't reply but slid from the berth. When her feet hit the floor, she adjusted the shawl around her shoulders and pulled it tight near her bosom with one hand. With the other, she reached up, grabbed the pistol, then shoved it in a side pocket in her nightdress.

The act didn't surprise Clive. Again, he would've done the same thing. But he clearly didn't have a huge understanding of women's nightwear. Although he'd removed many nightdresses from women in his time, he'd never known a female to secret something in a nightgown pocket.

He stood aside so she could walk before him. When

they reached the door, he slid it open and followed her outside.

His mind had gone from pockets to the woman beneath the nightwear. And what else beside a pistol hid beneath the demure white cotton…

****

Pansy had felt the calloused fist around her ankle an instant before she felt the cold, hard steel of what could only be a pistol dropped against her shin. She hadn't been sleeping, only resting, a fact that probably saved her from whatever the man thought to do to her.

She shook her head to clear it. No, she wouldn't allow herself to consider what the outcome would have been had she not been awake—and grabbed the pistol before the man had the opportunity to carry out his plan.

Mr. Cooper's sudden appearance had helped, too.

It hit her then that the man standing beside her on the metal platform showed up when she most needed assistance. Did he just have a knack for being in the right place at the right time, or was there more to it? Could the man be following her?

She took a step away and put a bit of distance between their bodies. Not that she could get much farther, given that her right hip already brushed the railing. Her nightdress sagged on that side, a reminder that the pistol hung near her thigh. No need to step away to use it, if necessary.

She wasn't above shooting a hole in her clothing if forced to do so.

"Are you okay?" The man's tone held concern, and when she turned to meet his gaze, it showed in his eyes. That she even entertained the idea he might be less than honorable shamed her. "I'm sorry that happened."

Her shoulder lifted, then fell. "It's not your fault."

"No, but I'm still sorry you had to go through that. No woman should be put in that kind of position." He removed his Stetson, held it loosely in one hand, and looked away. "I hate when men try to take advantage of women. It's not right."

A long, slow exhale to release some of the tension in her body. "No, it's not." She loosened her grip on the railing. "But when it does happen, it's a blessing to have a man like you around to lend a hand." She met his gaze. "I don't think I've thanked you yet…for everything, not just…" She waved a hand to the car behind them. "Not only what just happened, but for everything you've done for me. Thank you, Mr. Cooper. I am profoundly grateful."

For a long moment, the only sound, the clatter of iron wheels on railroad track, broke the silence. She thought he might not reply, but he finally shook his head. The corner of his lip curled up, and his eyes held amusement.

"I don't believe anyone has ever called me a blessing before. That, Miss Buchanan, is thanks enough."

Now she smiled. Conversation came easily with the man. It had been such a tedious task, speaking with Filly, but this wasn't anything like that experience. Words flowed between them without effort. He smiled at unexpected moments and put her even further at ease.

She had not realized it could be this way.

Don't get used to this. Her mind sent out a warning, but her body heated at the nearness of the man. She stepped closer.

"I can hardly believe that. Why, you've been

nothing but helpful since the moment we met." No need to fabricate anything. The truth came in a rush. "From the start almost of my journey, you've shown up when I needed someone. I don't think I can ever repay such kindness."

The man's lip tilted higher.

The scent of him, spice and tobacco, mingled with the odor of coal smoke and pine trees. The area beyond the tracks, cloaked in darkness, brought an intimacy to the moment. She imagined they must be passing a forest and inhaled as deeply as she could. It made her head spin, but only a very small bit and in the nicest way.

"Standing out here beneath the stars with me is repayment enough." His gaze dropped to her shoulders, where her hair lay undone, for an instant. He lifted his gaze and looked into her eyes, as if the stars were strewn across her expression rather than the expanse of violet black above them. "Although nothing in the heavens can hold a candle to your beauty."

Not something Mother would approve of, her standing in such a state with a man, but she had departed this world, and Pansy was the one deciding her fate now. And if she felt safe enough to share the sight of her disorganized state with this gentleman, so be it.

Because surely, despite his worn boots and the six-shooters he wore, he must be a gentleman. Not the kind she left behind, but a rugged, exciting version of the old standard. If he weren't, he would have certainly made a move to take advantage of her delicate nature, wouldn't he? Well, he hadn't, despite having several opportunities to do so, and that made him gentlemanly enough in her eyes.

And if she were to let the lovely romantic things he

said send a thrill up her spine, that was her business.

She should go inside, she knew that. Remove herself from this compromising position, off the swaying, clattering wood beneath her feet, and into the relative safety of her bunk.

But something in his eyes kept her rooted to her position. His words touched someplace deep inside her, a spot that longed for love and bloomed when he spoke this way.

It was temporary. And unreal, even. After tomorrow they'd never see each other again. So what harm could come of standing in the starlight and pretending this stranger thought highly of her?

None. The next depot drew closer with every passing minute. Their moments were limited. No one would be the wiser, and she would take this memory with her to whatever life lay ahead.

Pansy smiled. "You are too kind, Mr. Cooper." She gestured to the sky. "Why, those constellations would put any woman to shame. None can rival them, certainly."

"You're not saying I don't know beauty when I see it, are you?" His tone, so tender and deep, touched her soul.

She shook her head, conscious of the tangle of hair that fell over her breasts. "Not at all. I'm just thinking that you're stretching the truth a bit…"

"Well, I guess beauty really is in the eye of the beholder. And my eyes have no interest in looking at anything except what's standing in front of me." He lowered his voice, although there wasn't anyone around to hear them. A slight tilt forward from the hips brought his face closer. "And I have to be perfectly honest and tell you, I don't believe I've ever seen a woman look more fetching in the moonlight."

Her breath caught in her throat.

She should go inside. It would be the proper thing to do.

Mother had raised her four daughters to be good women. Women who didn't dawdle in the dark with strangers. Not even strangers who rescued them when they needed it.

No, she shouldn't stay out here with him.

Her conscience poked at her. Insistent.

But she pushed back, so hard that every thought about walking away from Clive Cooper vanished from her head. She followed her heart on this one and leaned closer the man.

So close, she could see the stubble on his chin. Near enough that the smell of coal smoke didn't get past the manly scents coming from his jacket. Scant inches separated them, so she tossed common sense over the railing.

And kissed him right on the lips.

For a fleeting second, his mouth didn't move. Then, he kissed her back.

Her arms came up around his shoulders when he placed a hand on her back and pulled her against his body. The strength of the man caught her off guard. His muscular form, so solid and immobile. It had been so long since she felt safe, but as they kissed, it was as if a protective wall rose around them, sheltering her from the rigors of the world.

His tongue slipped between her lips, a shock that both scandalized and intrigued her. She let him explore her mouth for an instant, then she trailed her own tongue across his lips and deeper. She had never imagined two people could kiss this way, but now that she knew, she gave herself to it wholeheartedly.

A moan escaped her lips, and she pushed closer to the man's form. Something hard pressed against her hip…not the revolver in her pocket and not the one holstered in his gun belt, either. A thrill sent quivers throughout her body, lighting fires in places that had never been touched by heat before. The feeling stole the breath from her body. Her mind became tangled, the only solid thought…getting closer to the man in her arms in the hope he'd know how to deal with the flames he'd lit.

He tightened his arms around her, and for a moment she thought she'd combust right on the spot. Then, he released her and took a big step back.

And she felt lost. Again.

"Miss Buchanan, I apologize." His voice rasped in the cool night air. "I shouldn't have taken liberties with you. I never should have kissed you that way."

Pansy's mind spun. Her body still yearned for his touch, yet it was clear that he had no intention of continuing their exchange.

Well, she wouldn't be made a fool of. Certainly, he'd realized her inexperience and had second thoughts about what they had been doing. There wasn't any other explanation for his suddenly stepping back. It didn't take a soiled dove to see that she'd excited him, even if only on a carnal level.

But her mother hadn't raised a fool.

She placed her hands in her pockets so she wouldn't be tempted to touch him again and took a step toward the door leading into the sleeper car.

A look over her shoulder to meet his gaze. His eyes

were dark, his hat shading them from view.

She swallowed hard, then spoke the truth. "You didn't kiss me, Mr. Cooper." She found the latch to open the door with her fingers. "I kissed you."

Chapter 5

Cheyenne wasn't anything like Pansy imagined it would be.

But then, maybe her timing put the town at a disadvantage. She hadn't thought to get off the train at the crack of dawn, but the altercation with the drunken stranger who attempted to climb into her bunk last night followed by her behavior with Clive Cooper just a short time later gave her few options. She figured the man whose six-shooter she carried in her bag would come looking for his property, probably sooner rather than later. When he did, he might remember how she'd treated him, and that just might make him less romantically inclined and bent on revenge instead. After all, he didn't seem like the type of fellow who would appreciate being bested by a woman.

And then there was the matter of Clive and the kiss…well, the memory of that moment sent heat flooding through her body in waves. Her mouth went dry, and she felt a flame in her cheeks. Gratitude for the darkness that concealed any sign of her thoughts, although there were few to witness her…

What was it, exactly? Not shame. She wasn't in the least bit ashamed of her behavior. Certainly, Mother flipped in her grave, but that couldn't be helped.

The kiss aboard the Union Pacific had been her first. As far as life experiences went, it shot to the top of her all-time best moments. If she died today, at least she'd been properly kissed by a man. A rugged, handsome man, at that.

If she had to put a finger on what she felt, what caused the burning on her cheekbones and warmth lower on her body, she would say excitement mingled with pride incited her reaction to the memory. She imagined any woman would be thrilled to kiss a man the way she had. And that, the fact that for one of the first times in her life she actually did what she wanted without guidance or approval from another person, made her proud. If she were to be on her own, she deserved the chance to think for herself. Which she had, when she kissed the man.

No way to blame her actions on anyone else. Not that she wanted to. It had taken her all of one second to decide to claim that man's lips, and if she had the chance, she'd do it again.

And again.

And that's why she made her way down the metal train steps in the near dark and collected her trunk while the rest of the travelers slept. She had to get clear of both men before they woke.

But as she looked around at the dusty, dirt water town, she wondered if she'd jumped into more trouble than dealing with either man would have been. Her trunk had been deposited on the wide wooden walkway near the tracks. She stepped over to it and dropped herself onto an edge.

The train pulled out of the station, sending a cloud of smoke into the air as its wheels churned up waves of red dust. Pansy should have held her breath for a minute while the mess settled, but she had so little experience standing beside trains that she didn't think to do so. She inhaled it all into her lungs and instantly felt her throat close.

Tears streamed from her eyes as she gagged. She turned her back on the tracks and gasped, but she'd waited too long. The smoke and dust choked her. Panic replaced all thoughts of independence, choosing her own fate, or even the physical response she'd discovered possible last night.

Now she hurried to the edge of the platform, leaned over, and retched. Spittle flew from her mouth like fire, burning all the way up her throat. Fortunately, it happened quickly, leaving sore ribs from the exertion and tingling lips. Lord, whoever would have thought a lungful of train smoke could hurt a person this way?

She straightened, wiped a shaky hand across her mouth, and looked around. The platform would probably be bustling in a few hours, but now, as the first fingers of sun peeked over the tops of buildings, only two other people shared the space. Embarrassment didn't hit as hard in the early morning light in a strange western town as it would have done had she still been in Charleston. Besides, some things could not be helped, including gagging after inhaling noxious fumes.

A woman could only endure so much, and she'd already put up with more than her share of bad luck.

Cheyenne ought to have been more inviting, as well. The fact that the place was the first city to allow a woman to sit on a jury should have been reason enough to put on a decent showing. Her gaze swept over every building in sight, and none impressed her one bit.

Why, the place didn't look much better than any of the countless other towns they'd blown by on the westward journey. Surely, it didn't even come close to being as polished as Chicago—and she'd been assaulted there. A rough place, still rebuilding after their big fire, but not so hard that the people there didn't at least offer some impression of welcoming newcomers.

She hadn't wanted to disembark in Cheyenne to begin with. Now that she had, she wished she'd taken her chances with the weaponless man and the other with the kissable lips.

Her behavior, undoubtedly, caught the attention of the couple standing a distance from her. The woman broke from the man with her and walked over. When she grew close, Pansy saw she, at least, looked respectable. A sensible gray traveling ensemble, dirty at the hem but otherwise impeccable, and a fashionable hat to match gave the sense that the other did not pose a risk but rather offered an opportunity to meet a woman similar to her own upbringing.

"I don't mean to pry, but are you unwell?" The woman's brows knitted together and gave her otherwise ordinary face some character.

Pansy guessed her to be a year or two older than she was and, as she'd thought, a morally sound person. Mousy brown hair pulled into a neat twist and so firmly anchored with several hairpins that she instantly recalled her eldest sister, Lily. The first sister had shown her siblings how to insert hairpins that wouldn't come undone no matter what they went through. Now, the thought of her sister made her sad. Lily, just another person who assumed her younger sister incapable of thinking for herself.

Well, she'd show them. Even if they never met again, it would count that Pansy took control of her life.

"I'm fine, thank you for enquiring." She waved a hand toward the edge of the platform where she'd so recently stood and been ill. "The fumes from the train got to me, is all. Not the most elegant way to arrive in town, I'm afraid."

The other woman nodded. "But not the most elegant town, is it?"

A kindred soul! So, she wasn't alone in her disappointment.

"Not what I hoped for, at any rate." Beyond the last rooftop the sun rose over a distant mountaintop. The terrain had grown so harsh and rugged as the hours riding the train passed. Now she didn't see anything that even vaguely reminded her of where she'd come from.

Good. The less she remembered about all she'd lost, the better.

"You were expecting something more civilized?" The other woman leaned close, sending the scent of lavender into the air between them. She lowered her voice to a conspiratorial whisper, although there wasn't anyone near to hear them. The only other person in sight, apart from a train employee who leaned against the depot doorjamb smoking a pipe, was the man who she'd been standing with when Pansy first noticed them. "I did, too. When we stepped off the train, I just about turned myself right around and climbed back on board." She jerked her head in the direction of the man. "But my husband Adam said we'd come this far, we had to give the place a chance. I know better'n to argue with him when he's got his mind made up, so I gave in. We stayed."

Well, that certainly offered hope. If women who dabbed lavender behind their ears and onto their wrists, the way Mother always did, lived in this desolate outpost, then surely she, too, could make a go of it. Her intention had been to get farther away from her past, maybe to Laramie or the coastline, even. But like her new acquaintance, men had influenced her actions…and here she stood, in a place as barren as she'd ever seen.

"How long have you lived in Cheyenne?"

"Oh, we don't live here in town."

Pansy pulled her brows together. Maybe traveling for so long had tampered with her hearing. "But I thought you said your husband said you should stay here. And you said you stayed, didn't you?"

A slow nod as the woman clasped her hands at her waist. "Oh, he did. And I did." She closed her eyes and shuddered. She opened them and met Pansy's gaze. Her eyes had a steely glint. "But I didn't say we'd stayed here. No, this godforsaken town is no place for a woman. Did you know they lynched men not so long ago? That's right, lynchings right in the town itself. Not out in the plains, necktie justice where no 'un would see, but in plain view for folks to gather—like they was havin' a party! No, this isn't a place for women."

She'd heard about the lynchings. The news had made the papers all the way back home. But honestly, she expected lawlessness and the repercussions of criminal behavior to be harsh. The punishment didn't seem that far removed from a bullet in a shoot off outside a saloon, something she also expected took place. But she kept her thoughts to herself, especially since the other woman looked so scandalized by the event.

"Ah, yes. I'd heard something about that." She tipped her head toward the two men. They'd begun speaking, and while they were too far away to hear their words, neither looked ready to shoot the other. "Then if you don't live in Cheyenne, where do you live? Oh, I don't mean to be nosey, it's just that there doesn't seem to be too many options once you get off the train."

An understatement. Aside from the town, endless stretches of scrubby, tumbleweed-strewn plains surrounded them. In the far distance, a mountain range. Very few options for someone looking to make a new home.

A feeling of unease crept over Pansy. Maybe she should have stayed on the train. At least there she had other people to take her mind off her dilemmas. So far, the choices she'd made for herself had landed her in a spot that didn't offer much by way of encouragement.

Maybe I should have remained in Charleston. At least there I wasn't all alone.

"Oh, we moved to Wylder."

Wylder.

She had planned to peek at the town when the train passed through. And she'd intended to keep riding, all the way to Laramie or maybe even farther if that town didn't appear promising. She would go all the way to the ocean if she had to.

"Do you like living in Wylder?" She would have liked to ask whether this woman knew the town's schoolteacher but swallowed the question. No need to alert anyone of her presence or give someone a reason to wonder why she enquired about a teacher when she very obviously didn't have any children to enroll in school.

"Oh, we do. A much nicer place than Cheyenne." The other woman tilted her head to the side. "Is anyone in town expecting you? I can't help but notice that no one's come to greet you."

Pansy shook her head. "No, no one's waiting on me

here. I just…" She just what? The truth wasn't an option. "I just needed to get out and stretch my legs, is all. I plan to wait for the next train and keep moving westward."

"Well, that'll be a mighty long wait."

"Excuse me?" The time between trains in Chicago had been a few hours. She would sit on this platform and watch the sun rise. A sturdy wooden bench sat beside the wall behind her. It didn't look comfortable, but it would suffice. Maybe by the time the next train arrived, she would have a better plan in place about her future. Or at the very least, her imminent future. "I don't mind waiting."

The other woman shook her head and raised her voice, as if Pansy were either deaf or stupid. "You're not gettin' me, honey. This ain't New York or Atlanta, or wherever else you're from." She waved a finger at the railroad tracks. "That there track isn't gonna see another set of iron wheels for almost a week. Trains don't run nonstop in the west, the way you expect them to back in the old states." She crossed her arms and gave a sympathetic click with her tongue. "The life you knew back east? Well, it's over. It just don't exist anymore, and the sooner you realize it, the better off you'll be."

She'd be stuck in Cheyenne a week.

"A week?" Her voice sounded scratchy, so she cleared her throat. "Surely there must be another way to get out of this place. A stagecoach, perhaps? Some other means of transportation heading west?"

The other woman smiled. When she did, Pansy saw again a steely glint in her eyes. "Well, now, you are in luck…"

****

The couple introduced themselves as Cora and

Adam Masterson. When they offered Pansy a ride to Wylder, she didn't refuse.

Adam hoisted her trunk onto the bed of the wagon as if it were filled with feathers instead of all her worldly possessions. The man didn't appear that strong, but she supposed that living in the frontier must toughen a body.

He walked around to the two horses attached to the wagon. A pat for each, and a tug on the leather holding them in place.

The hard, wide wooden seat could accommodate the three of them. When Cora climbed into place and scooted close to Adam, Pansy put a foot on the closest wheel and hoisted herself up. Her shoulder bumped the other woman's.

"Sorry." She scooched until a few inches showed between them. Then she sat, placed her bag between her feet, and arranged her skirt. Days in the traveling outfit and hardly any sleep left her spine feeling tired, but she forced herself to sit upright anyway. Mother didn't raise her to be a slouch-shouldered woman. "I appreciate the ride. I don't know what I'd do if I had to stay in Cheyenne for a whole week."

Cora reached over and patted her hand. She noticed the calloused, dry skin and wondered what a woman had to do to get hands so work worn. While her life in Charleston hadn't been without its share of tasks, especially when her parents took ill, she had never done labor of the kind that would bring such roughness to her skin.

"Nothing to fret over. Gettin' inta a wagon after settin' on a train for days on end can't be easy." Now that they were rolling away from the train station, her speech took on a coarser tone. "No, I daresay it's gotta be hard to get your legs back under yourself after a ride like that."

Adam hadn't said a word when he climbed onto the wagon. He simply gave the horses the command to move and kept his gaze focused on the track ahead of them. The animals plodded along, not nearly as spritely as the ones Father kept at their place. So much for her to learn here, from the difference in horseflesh right up to…well, who could tell?

Best to try to glean all she could from the start.

"It was a tiring journey." Pansy glanced past the woman beside her, then returned her gaze to meet the tired gray eyes. "Where do you and Adam come from?"

The man cleared his throat.

Beside her, a stiffening, almost as if the pair communicated without words.

"Well, me an' Adam joined up with a wagon train just this side of…ah, Missouri. Just outside a' Missouri, that's it."

The way the woman hesitated made Pansy suspicious. How could she not know where they'd begun their journey west?

"A wagon train? Why, that must be even more arduous than traveling by rail train."

"It weren't easy, I'll tell ya that much."

Very evident now, that Cora had passed herself off as more refined when they had spoken on the platform. It didn't bother Pansy that the woman tried to put on airs. Back home, women did that all the time.

It worried her that she gave the impression that she deserved anyone going to that trouble. Part of her journeying westward on her own, without a chaperone or companion, included keeping up the appearance of being a very ordinary woman. Not the kind whose father had kept her in relative ease. No, she wanted to seem less a pampered youngest daughter and more like someone who could take on anything the west could throw her way.

I'll have to work harder on fitting in.

The day's heat already made itself known. Now that the sun rose above the distant mountain peaks, the air warmed. Every breath felt like an inhale from the devil's own personal playground. A trickle of sweat snaked down Pansy's back, turning the stiff cotton damp and reminding her of the horrid way she'd felt back in the hot Charleston park when she had taken a final leave of Filbert Snowe.

Filly.

The thought of him made her cringe. How could she have ever wasted time with the man? He lacked substance, and now that there were so many miles between them, she saw so much more clearly now than she had before.

Also, since she had made the acquaintance of a real man, one who knew how to stand up for a woman while still showing he respected her as more than a female, but as a person with the ability to make her own decisions. In their time together, Clive Cooper had never tried to inflict his opinions on her. Not once. So far, the only person she'd known who gave her that courtesy.

Clive. The name rolled around in her mind, a sweet sound tumbling against the inside of her head.

A shiver ran up her spine. She trembled, thinking about the feel of his lips on hers. Heat touched her cheeks and other places, too.

"Are you okay?" Cora nudged her with an elbow. "You're not takin' sick, are ya?"

Pansy drew her brows together. "No, I'm not unwell. Why do you ask?"

"Well, you've been shakin' right here beside me. I thought it might be the pox or somethin'."

The pox.

Horror swept through her. A sheen of perspiration broke out on her upper lip, so she wiped it away with the back of one hand.

"See? You're shiverin' and shakin' ag'in. Should we stop?"

Adam leaned forward. His expression didn't show compassion, but annoyance. She rushed to reassure them. The last thing she needed, to be stranded in the wilderness alone if they left her here. Surely it would kill her.

"No, please don't stop. I'm fine—really, I am." She swallowed and pushed the memories threatening to flood her mind away. The scenes of her parents' final moments, courtesy of the dreaded pox, were never far. "It's just…" She swallowed again. "Bad memories, is all. I lost someone dear to sickness a while back. It's…well, it's still hard. But I'm not unwell, I promise."

Cora patted her hand again as her husband settled back against the wood slat behind them.

"That's good to hear. No one wants to get sick out here in the frontier." She paused, then nodded toward the endless space beyond the trail. "No tellin' how many die out yonder on that red dirt, leavin' their bones for the sun to turn to dust."

Time to change the subject. "If you don't mind my asking, why were you in Cheyenne this morning? You must've left very early to meet the train."

Adam cleared his throat again. And Cora stiffened

beside him once more.

"Ah, why was we in town?" The other woman smoothed a hand over her skirt. A rasping sound accompanied the motion. "Well, it's like this…we was takin' a neighbor to meet the train on account he had a family emergency." Another sweep of her hand over her skirt. Then, she poked at a loose thread with a fingertip. "Unexpected, ya see. Wasn't expectin' to have to go west the way he did."

The hairs on the back of Pansy's neck stood up. She didn't know how she knew it, but she was certain the other woman lied. She scrambled to find something to say that wouldn't let on that she didn't believe one word of what she'd just been told.

"Well, that's mighty nice of you both, to do a neighbor a good turn that way."

As she spoke, Adam pulled back on the reins and halted the horses. They were far from anywhere, away from other people or buildings, so she couldn't figure out why they'd stopped moving.

Pansy glanced at their surroundings. Desolate, with tumbleweeds dotting the landscape. The only sign of life, a stand of cottonwoods to the right of the track.

A figure on horseback emerged from the trees. A second, riderless horse followed, but that wasn't what sent her heart thudding in her chest. She reached for Cora's hand and grabbed it. She squeezed, trying to pull the fear that swept through her under control.

The man looked unlike any other she'd met. Long black hair tied by a leather strip hung over his shoulder. A blue cotton shirt and denim trousers. Dusty leather moccasins on his feet. A black Stetson on his head.

When he drew close, he pinned her with his gaze.

The deepest brown eyes she'd ever seen, so dark they looked like night. His complexion, a beautiful bronze. Features so rugged and handsome, she couldn't look away.

She had known there were native people living in the west, but she hadn't thought to come face-to-face with one this quickly. Maybe eventually, in town or in the distance. But here? In a wagon with a couple she'd only just met?

Their options were limited. No place to run, nowhere to hide.

The newcomer raised his arm and pointed to her. "Get down from that wagon."

Nearly turned to stone from fear, she didn't move. Could this really be happening?

Adam lifted the reins as if to slap them against the horses, but the rider must have anticipated that because he kicked his mount's flanks and positioned himself right in front of them.

"Now look, we don't want no trouble from ya." Adam's voice wavered on the words.

Pansy glanced over at him and saw his chin shook. Beside her, Cora's face had gone white. Her lips pursed, and her eyes were shiny, as if she held back tears.

She turned her attention back to the native and saw no fear. The man sat tall astride his horse, as solid and unwavering as the mountain in the distance. A product of the land, rather than a newcomer drawn here to settle. She saw the difference between them, a stark contrast that showed the divide between those who settled the plains and others who were born from them.

The man's gaze met hers. Again, the dark eyes mesmerized her. "Get down from that wagon."

A number of frightening images flashed through her mind. She'd heard tales of women being carried off by natives to never be seen again. The horror of what might happen if she got out of the wagon kept her rooted to the hard wooden seat.

Cora spoke to her husband in a near-whisper. "Mebbe if he takes her, he'll let us go."

"It's what I'm hopin'."

So, her newfound friends were ready to hand her over to this stranger!

The native moved his horse closer. He pointed to her, then the ground beside the wagon. "Down. Now." His tone had grown harsher, and it sent Pansy's insides swirling. She hadn't eaten since yesterday, and she was glad for it. Surely if there'd been anything in her belly, she would lose its contents.

The man looked over at Adam. "Take her trunk off the wagon."

Adam didn't need to be told twice. He jumped down and ran to the back of the wagon. The sound of her trunk sliding over the worn wood, then thumping against the hard-packed trail, met her ears. When he'd dropped her trunk to the ground, the man climbed back into place and picked up the reins.

The native walked his horse closer to the side of the wagon, near its big front wheel. His gaze swept over all three of its occupants. It landed on her, and again, her blood ran cold.

Her options were limited. A rifle lay across the horse behind the saddle. If she refused, he might shoot her. But if she went with him, her fate might be worse. Strange to think that only a few months ago, she never would have believed there could be a fate worse than death, but she did now.

The decision whether to exit the wagon as the man ordered went from her power in a heartbeat. Cora appeared petite and accommodating, but she had no reluctance when she gave Pansy a shove. The move came unexpectedly. Shock was the woman's ally, because almost the instant she realized what had happened, Pansy flew from the seat toward the ground.

Rocks bit into her palms when she hit the trail. She landed beside the wagon, in front of the horse and rider. Her bag sat a few feet from her, so she reached for it and pulled it to her chest.

She shot a hard look at Cora, but again, the woman avoided her gaze. The set of her mouth, in a tight, thin line told her story. She wanted to survive and didn't care if she had to sacrifice another woman to make it happen.

The sound of leather hitting flesh a scant second before the wagon wheels began to creak and roll stole the breath from her lungs. It was actually happening, this thing that every well-bred southern woman had been warned happened on the western frontier. She'd been taken prisoner by a native and would probably be violated, scalped, and killed—and there was little she could do about it.

Except look for her chance to shoot at the bastard, the way she'd done with the man on the train. This time, though, she would have to do more than fire a warning shot. She would have to hit this man to stop him, she felt sure of it.

The under-over derringer in her skirt pocket might work, but if she could find a chance to get to the six-shooter she'd taken from the last man who had tried to assault her, she could surely kill the native.

Now, she knelt with her bag clutched to her chest. A look toward the dust trail left by the disappearing wagon. Then, she raised her chin and met the man's eyes. They were so dark that she couldn't get a feel for his intentions. His features had softened a little, which she took as a good sign.

"Get up." He spoke English with precision. When she didn't move, he brought the horse a few steps closer. "I said get up."

She looked around. The frontier stretched on without any sign of humanity. Dusty, red soil. Tumbleweeds. Mountain range in the distance. Scattered clusters of cottonwoods.

What choice did she have?

Pansy pushed to her feet. Her landing from the wagon had been hard. Her knees hurt, and one ankle protested when she stood. Nothing terrible, just a body saying it had been misused.

The man held a hand out to her. She stared at it. His fingers were long and his palm, wide and calloused. A strong, dark hand, one that looked as if it could crush her if he chose to do so. Men in the south didn't offer hands like this one to ladies. In truth, the palm had a rugged beauty to it that had she not been suffering from shaking knees and mind-numbing fright, would have intrigued her.

But she stared. Evidently, for too long because the man leaned down and shook his hand near her face. "We need to go. Now."

A decision to be made, hers alone to make it. If she refused, she figured he would carry her off screaming. But if she went peacefully, she might be able to catch a moment to turn the situation to her benefit. The six-shooter could change everything, if only she found the right time to use it. And if she could take it from her bag without him realizing what she intended to do.

Pansy took a deep breath, then put her hand in his.

One fast tug sent her flying through the air toward the space behind him. When her bottom landed on the horse, she swung one leg over to sit astride. Not enough room to keep any distance from the man, so her body snugged up against his. He hadn't let go of her hand, and now he pulled it around his waist and waited while she situated herself. Her bag fit between them if she slid a few inches back, so she did. His fingers tightened on hers.

"Hold on."

He tapped the horse, and they began to ride. It hit her then that her trunk stood in the trail and would probably be taken by the next person who passed. All of her possessions were gone.

The horse moved faster, and even though the native held her hand against his hard belly, she nearly slid off. No sense falling again, so she slipped her other arm around the man and took hold of her other wrist.

He loosened his grip on her fingers and took his hand away.

Then he did something that shocked her.

He ran a slow fingertip over her knuckles, so tenderly that it could have been a lover's caress.

Chapter 6

Pansy took a deep breath and lunged again. Her shoulders screamed in protest, and the rope binding her wrists to each other cut into her flesh, but she threw her entire weight into the move and prayed the ropes would break.

No such luck. She leaned back against the raspy bark of the cottonwood and let her knees fold. She slid to the ground, her breath coming in gasps as if she'd been running. She gulped for air, not even minding that it felt hotter than the steam coming off a cast-iron skillet. A sheen of perspiration covered her forehead, but she could not wipe it away. It stung her eyes, but she blinked to clear them.

The native had left her in a cluster of trees. Branches stretched toward the sky, so tall they seemed endless when she tipped her head back. At least they provided shade against the sun and offered some measure of protection against the day's heat.

What the man lacked in conversational skills he made up for in his ability to tie knots. He'd roped her to the tree without uttering a word. And she was certain that the strongest frontier storm wouldn't be able to blow her away. As long as the cottonwood stood, she'd be at its base.

There went her hope of making it on her own, being the one behind her life decisions and finding her way in the world. Before she had the chance to make one important decision, she'd had her reticule stolen, been put upon by a drunk on a train, nearly seduced by a man whose lips were so tender they made her knees weak, and now this. How to even come to terms with dying at the hands of a tomahawk-wielding wild man?

Although she hadn't seen any tomahawks. The only weapon the man carried, that she could tell, was the rifle. It looked well-worn, the wood scarred. But he hadn't touched it in her presence.

And to his credit, he didn't seem wild. Not in any dangerous sort of way, that is.

Oh, what was she thinking? The man had tied her to a tree and left her to die. How could he not be considered wild? No man back east, leastways none she knew, would even consider tying a woman to anything, let alone a tree in the wilderness.

Another hard thrust forward confirmed her suspicions about his rope-tying talents. Unless she somehow figured out how to chew the ropes and free herself, she wasn't going anywhere.

Better to wait and see if he returned. Maybe if he did, he'd release her.

And if he didn't…

She looked over her left shoulder, then the right. There must be all kinds of animals out here, and with the obvious lack of vegetation, she imagined they must be hungry.

Good Lord, but she didn't want to become a meal for a predator!

****

Pansy woke to the touch of someone—or something—sliding along the skin about her wrist.

Snake?

Snake!

Fear shot through her as a scream escaped her throat. "No!"

She scrabbled to get to her feet, but as she pushed herself off the ground, tingles sped up her legs. From calves to thighs, spasms in muscles that had gone to sleep during the hours she had dozed. They didn't hold, and her knees buckled. She hit the ground hard, jerking on her arms that were still wrapped behind her around the tree trunk. Her wrists screamed in protest, a fresh jolt of searing pain as the rope cut deeper into her tender skin.

"Oh, damn it all!" Her head whipped around, her gaze searching the nearby ground for any sign of the creature that woke her. The snake wasn't in sight, but that didn't mean he had slithered away.

"Hold still."

The male voice behind her sounded familiar. For a second, she had forgotten her situation. But now, as she sat folded on hard ground with her heart hammering in her chest and her arms trussed behind her as if she were a Thanksgiving turkey, she remembered.

Captive. I am held hostage by a savage.

Only his touch, now that she realized he wasn't a snake, didn't feel savage. Not at all. The fingers that brushed her skin as they worked on the knots in the rope were gentle. The tension holding her hands together loosened. The man placed his hand on her arm, just above her right wrist, and held her in place as he released the knot. His grip kept her from falling forward. As he guided her hand around the tree, she settled onto her backside and hugged her arms to her chest. A length of rope trailed from her left wrist, but she ignored it.

He came around from the other side of the cottonwood and stood for a moment before her. She refused to look up and concentrated on rubbing her thighs to get blood circulating again. The pins-and-needles sensation faded a little bit more with each passing moment.

The man squatted, bringing his gaze level with hers. He looked down to her thighs where her hands still massaged, then back up into her face. "I'm sorry I startled you that way."

Sorry he startled her? How about sorry he kidnapped her?

The words were on the tip of her tongue, but she feared angering him if she spoke them. So she nodded and kept her lips pressed firmly together.

He waited a moment, then tipped his head toward her left wrist. "If you lift your hand, I'll remove the rope."

She raised her arm and flipped her hand over so he could gain access to the knot. Her wrist showed evidence of her attempts to escape. A dark band of red, raw skin circled her wrist. When the rope fell away, she pulled her hand to her breast. God, but it hurt!

"Think you can stand yet?"

Pansy ignored the hand he offered. She put one of hers on the ground and used the other to tug her skirt out from under her feet. When she felt reasonably sure she wouldn't trip over her clothing, she pressed her back against the tree and straightened her legs. They held, but she swayed when the world began to spin.

The native put a steadying hand on her upper arm. His touch was strong, but gentle, too. "Easy. Give it a minute." She wanted to push him away, but his grasp and the tree behind her were the only things that felt solid. "You slept all day. No food or water, that's the problem. You'll feel better after you eat."

After I eat?

In the hours before sleep claimed her, she'd imagined all kinds of horrible things that could befall her now that she had been taken prisoner. Stories of what happened to white women at the mercy of natives on the frontier hadn't gone unnoticed. She knew what uncivilized men did to innocent women.

Why would he feed her before ravishing her body?

Maybe he wanted her to have some stamina for whatever lay ahead of her. He might expect her to dance for him or perform some other godawful mating ritual.

Well, she'd eat. But not to please him. If she were to escape, she would need energy to do so.

"Can you walk? Has your head stopped spinning yet?"

His voice, so deep and strong it calmed her nerves. Then she realized the effect he was having and met his gaze. "You speak English."

One corner of his upper lip lifted. A lopsided grin, then a shoulder shrug. The cotton shirt he wore pulled against his form, revealing muscular shoulders and biceps.

"You sound surprised."

"I thought you, ah…" How to not insult the man who held her life in his hands? A fast swallow gave her a second to think. "I have been under the impression that your people don't speak much English, if any at all. I believed you have your own language."

He looked at her for what felt like forever before he spoke. His eyes, so dark they appeared bottomless, hid his thoughts when she forced herself to meet his gaze. There were times for turning away from a stare that would be considered rude under different circumstances. This was not the time to stand on adherence to manners or social protocol.

Finally, he spoke. "We do have our own language, but I learned to speak the white man's words, as well."

"Why?" She couldn't keep the question from tumbling from her mouth.

Fortunately, he didn't seem annoyed by her rudeness. Another thoughtful look kept her still. It hit her that the man intrigued her and she truly wanted to know more about him, especially his feelings toward those who joined his people in the west.

"I knew a white man once who did my family a good turn. When I met him, I knew very little of the language of your people." He took a deep breath, as if steeling himself to speak the next words. "It came to pass that I am indebted to the man. The best way to return his favor is by helping his people. And I can't do that if I can't communicate with them." He studied her for another long minute. Then he smoothed his hand down her upper arm to her elbow. She'd forgotten he still held her until his fingers gave her a tiny squeeze. "Now, do you think you're ready to eat something?"

He stepped back and held out an arm. Beyond the tree, in the clearing, he'd built a small fire. The scent of cooking reached her nose, and her mouth watered.

"Yes, thank you."

So, maybe he wasn't as savage as she'd believed. And if she were lucky, he wouldn't cook her and eat her, like natives did in some of the stories she'd heard.

His arm held steady, and she realized he waited for

her to precede him to the fire. Was it politeness that kept him from leading the way? Or did he realize that she entertained the idea of bashing him over the head with a rock and stealing his horse?

Whatever the reason, he held her captive. Her options were limited, so she nodded her head and went to the fire. She sat near it, on the same side from where the man's horses stood tied beneath a cottonwood tree.

Her captor squatted by the fire. Two metal dishes sat on large rocks at the edge of the ring of flames. They each held some kind of stew and a hunk of cornbread. He passed one to her, along with a spoon.

"You will feel better after you eat."

She accepted the plate and sniffed the contents. It smelled divine. There wasn't much stew served at her parents' home, but what had been on the table smelled nothing like this. Fresh, with the pungent aroma of herbs, the mix of vegetables in sauce made her mouth water. She slid a potato onto her spoon and brought it to her mouth.

Sheer heaven.

Food had never tasted this good. She nodded her appreciation and began to eat. The man did the same, and the only sounds breaking the silence were the spoons against the metal plates.

She watched him from beneath half-lowered lids, wondering just how savage he might be. So far, he had shown no sign of wanting to take her hair or violate her person, but that could change in an instant. She had always been envious of her sister Daisy's long, lush curls but was now grateful that her own locks weren't nearly as beautiful. She hoped his kind didn't fancy ordinary heads of hair because she definitely wanted to keep hers—both the head and the hair.

If he knew she watched him, he didn't let on. And, if he kept an eye on her, he did it without giving himself away. She felt sure he did watch her, even if just to keep her from running off.

Well, he could think her a helpless white female all he wanted. When the chance came to bolt, she would take it. And, if she could figure out how to do it, she planned to take his horses, too. Both of them.

"Want more?" His words startled her.

She looked down at her empty plate. He had given her a substantial portion of stew. How had she eaten it all without realizing?

A fast head shake. "No." When he tilted his head and gestured to the pot, she added, "No, thank you." It wouldn't do to get so full that she couldn't run.

The man tipped the rest of the stew onto his plate. Now that she had finished, he openly surveyed her while he ate.

Disconcerting, to be examined in such a way. She felt like a bug on the end of a pin in a schoolroom. Was he looking for flaws in her structure? Or did his curiosity make him behave badly?

Maybe if she showed she didn't fear him, he wouldn't think her at his mercy. "That's rude, you know." She swept a hand down her skirt. It had dirt on its front, and she had no idea what the back looked like, but she could at least try to find her dignity. If Mother were here, she'd insist upon her daughter doing her best to stay presentable. When he continued to watch her, she shook her head. "Staring. It is rude to stare like that."

A slow grin spread across the man's face. Handsome when he smiled. So much so that her own lips twitched as they began to return the gesture. But she recalled their situation, so she gave her mouth what she hoped was a stern expression.

"Where are you from?"

The question was so direct it left little room for wiggling. Still, she'd be damned before she'd let him interrogate her.

"Back east."

His grin widened. "Figured as much. The train comes through east to west, don't it?"

"Doesn't it." The words were out of her mouth in a flash. She held her breath, hoping he didn't offend easily.

His laughter surprised her as much as her thoughtless words had.

"You must be a schoolteacher."

She pondered. There were few callings she could consider herself qualified for. Certainly, schoolteacher wasn't one of them, but she'd seen enough of Violet's life to maybe convince him otherwise.

"That's right. I'm a schoolteacher, and there are people waiting on me. When I don't arrive, they'll come looking." She swallowed hard and waved a hand toward the trees behind her. "After all, the schoolchildren can't be left to teach themselves, can they?"

He tipped his head back. The last of the day's sunrays peeked over the tops of the tall trees surrounding them. When he dropped his chin to look at her, his gaze held amusement.

For an instant she thought of showing her annoyance. Then, she remembered he had the advantage. Armed and stronger, someone to incite caution.

"Where are these children who wait for you?"

"Wylder. I am going to Wylder to teach at the

school." She held his gaze and raised her chin, inviting him to call her bluff. "And they are waiting on me, so you'd best let me go."

He had finished his meal and laid his plate to the side. Now he picked up a stick and tossed it onto the fire. "Well, Miss Schoolteacher, you will be happy to know you're already in Wylder."

Her brow furrowed. How could that be?

"I don't believe you."

"Didn't expect you to. After all, I am not a white man, like the one you were riding with, am I?" He threw another piece of wood on the fire, sending the flames high. In the firelight, his skin took on a deeper cast. "If I were a white man, you would believe me, the way you did with the one who was cartin' you off to sell to other white men."

Sell? Her mouth went dry. Surely she misunderstood him.

For a minute the only sound was the fire's crackling.

Finally, she found her voice. "Did you say 'sell'?"

A nod sent his hair whispering along his shoulder. "I did. That couple you were with? They take women who land out here with no one to meet them at the train station and bring them to other men who pay them for the women." He ran a hand across his chin, as if saying the words pained him. "White men selling white women to men who need women. That is what your people are doing, and no one is stopping it. If it were my people stealing white women and selling them for brides, there would be hell to pay."

Fear sliced through Pansy like a hot knife. Good Lord, what kind of place was this?

"Why did you stop them?" Her throat had gone so

dry the words were a whisper.

The man turned his gaze from the fire to her. She saw compassion in the dark eyes, almost as if he felt her fear and wished to comfort her with a look. But that couldn't be, could it? From what she had heard, these native people didn't have any kind feelings for white settlers.

He shrugged and gave her a half smile. "It is not our way, to treat women as if they have no value. The white man's coin? That is not fair exchange for a woman. The females in my tribe are the heart of our homes. They bring forth life, care for the crops, tend to the old ones. They are not to be sold for silver." He shook his head. "And I do not believe the white man's women are as worthless as they seem to think."

"You kept me from being sold?"

"It is not right, to sell a woman."

He looked toward the lowering sun, as if the conversation had come to its natural conclusion. And in a way, she guessed it had.

So, he'd saved her from being sold. But that didn't mean his plans for her were without danger. She'd keep her eyes open and wait. He had to put his guard down eventually. When he did, she would run like the hounds of hell were on her heels.

****

Beyond the circle of light cast by the fire, a darkness so complete it looked as if it could swallow a person. Pansy swept her gaze from the face of the man seated across from her to the gloom, then back again. He had been silent since their dinner conversation, and that suited her fine. It gave her time to think, to make a plan, and watch for any sign he might be thinking of doing her

109

harm.

She had the under-over derringer in her pocket and still hadn't figured out a way to get the other revolver from her bag. If she went for her things, she felt sure he'd look inside the satchel before allowing her access. He wasn't stupid. He must know that if she had a weapon hidden, she would go for it.

So rather than lose the six-shooter, she comforted herself with the thought that her derringer would stop a man if she aimed well. The means to success with a firearm, Father had told all his daughters, came not through strength but intelligence. Shoot wisely and reap the rewards had been his advice.

She planned to shoot wisely. That is, if he forced her to do so. If she could get away without killing the native, she'd be just as happy.

He stood, walked to the horses, and removed a blanket roll. As he returned to the circle of firelight, he separated two blankets and handed one to her. She took it, expecting a scratchy woolen length of fabric, but her fingers dug into a soft, but sturdy, woven creation. She pulled it onto her lap and ran a hand over the colorful design. A dark blue background showcased rows of red, ombre, forest green, and yellow figures dancing across the fabric.

"The fire will keep us warm." His voice cut the stillness. "But you will need something to cover yourself to keep the morning dampness from seeping in."

She looked up at him. He remained standing a foot away.

"Thank you." A quick look toward the darkness, then back to meet his gaze. "You said we're in Wylder. But I don't see a town, so how can that be?"

He raised an arm and pointed. Since she couldn't see anything beyond the firelight, he could be gesturing in any direction. "The town is over there, about a mile or so. This is Wylder, but beyond the area where your people are living. They consider it part of their settlement, this section of the plains." His face remained neutral, but his words had a bite to them. "What the white man sees, he takes."

Land disputes had been part of the news she'd read about before coming west. Settlers claimed the land was up for grabs while the natives asserted their tribes had lived on the frontier long before the first white man appeared. It seemed to her that there wasn't any good way to resolve something like that, where both parties insisted they owned the same thing.

Well, now that she had a vague idea on which direction the town sat, she thought it wise to change the subject. Best not to get the man angry, not when she still had no notion what he planned to do with—or to—her.

"This blanket is beautiful." She covered her lap with the fabric and ran a hand over the figures. "It's so soft, and the details are woven into the fabric. I'm amazed by the workmanship."

He squatted and reached a hand out to touch the blanket. "My mother made it. And the figures tell a story."

"She is incredibly talented, to do such fine work as this." Curiosity got the best of her. What started as a ploy to calm him turned into something more. How could any woman do such detailed work by weaving rather than stitching? "I could never do anything this intricate. Where I come from, I learned to embroider stories and images onto fabric rather than weave them into it. This is stunning."

"She is a very capable woman, my mother."

"Would you tell me what the figures signify?" After the words left her mouth, she wondered if the request might insult him. And, after insulting, anger the man. "That is, unless you don't want to tell me. Really, I don't mean to be rude."

He met her gaze. The darkness shielded the expression in his eyes, but his words brought relief. They were soft, and kind, and not at all insulted.

"It is an honor to speak of my mother's creation." He pointed to a figure and chuckled. "This is my story, as my mother tells it. When I was a young one, I did not listen as well as I should have. On this day, I wandered away." He pointed to a teepee, then to a wiggly blue line. "I left home, where I had been told to play with my brothers and sisters, and went to the stream. I followed the water, splashing in the shallow pools and looking to catch a fish." A finger traced the line until it touched a woven fish. "I could not catch the fish, it was too fast, so I went farther, into a forest." A stand of trees showed clearly on the blue background. "By then, Grandfather Moon had called Grandmother Sun to sleep, and darkness fell. Stars lit the night sky, but the young explorer could not find his way home."

A little boy lost!

"So what happened?"

He pointed to a small figure hunkered beneath a tree. "I sat with the night." He traced a slender line of light coming from a star above the child's shoulder. "And followed it to greet the day." A few inches farther, a small group of people, with the child being held aloft.

"You were found."

A nod. "I was." His fingertip lovingly traced the figure of a woman. "My mother would not allow the story to end differently."

Pansy considered her own mother's reaction to anything similar. If any of her girls had gotten lost in the night, surely she would have turned Charleston on its head searching for them. Yet the mother figure on the woven blanket wore a smile.

"Was your mother angry?"

He gazed at the blanket for a long moment. She wondered if she'd asked a question that didn't sit well with him because by the way he pursed his lips, he didn't look like an answer would come. But with a shake of his head, he met her gaze. The dark eyes sparkled, and the corners of his lips finally turned upward.

"My mother did not get angry. Instead, she held me high and danced. She said that one who knows the earth and is unafraid to wander freely is one who will travel with confidence." He ran a lazy fingertip over the figures before pulling his hand back. "I am grateful for a mother who knew that the earth would protect her son. That is the kind of woman I wish to mother my own children, one who knows that this land is home to our people. And our home, it shelters us."

His faith in the land surprised her. All she'd heard about this wilderness, with its storms, lawlessness, and rugged, unforgiving terrain did not instill confidence that it would keep anyone—especially not a child—safe.

"Aren't you afraid of wild animals?" His eyes widened, but Pansy pressed him. "There are creatures out here that would harm an innocent child. Why, there must be mountain lions and coyotes…all manner of untamed beasts."

Despite the heat from the fire, a chill swept over her. The friendly banter, with its smiles and shimmering eyes, disappeared.

Now the man's eyes turned even darker, and his stare turned her mouth dry. Had she crossed the line? Insulted him by questioning his mother's beliefs?

Had the time come for him to turn from the one who saved her to someone who would do her harm?

His words dripped ice. "The only creatures here now that my people need to worry will do us harm are the white men. They steal and kill without remorse." He stood, so she tipped her head back. Darkness hid his features, but she didn't need to see his face to know his heart. "I would sooner trust a hungry bobcat than a well-fed white man. Have you forgotten what your people have done to you? If I hadn't stopped them on the trail, you would be in the bed of a paleface who thinks your life is worth a few coins. And when he tired of you…well, let's just say you would be better off facing the wolf than the white man."

She watched him turn and walk to the far side of the fire. He didn't stop, though. His footsteps were silent, soft leather moccasins making no sound as they trod the red dirt. When the darkness swallowed his form, Pansy spread the blanket on the ground. She wrapped it around her and tucked her knees up against her chest.

She didn't know the man's name, had only met him this very day, but deep in her heart she knew he told the truth. The Wyoming territory wasn't Charleston, and for the first time since beginning her travels, she wondered if this decision would prove to be the death of her.

How could she survive in a land where wild animals were tame by comparison to men?

Chapter 7

Her dirty traveling dress, with its cotton underskirt and her long underpants, saved her knees when the toe of her leather shoe caught on a rock and sent her flying. Again. Hands met gravel, and dust flew up into her face. The bite of a stone on her shin made her suck in a breath, but she didn't cry out.

No, that would draw attention, and the last thing she wanted was to alert the night creatures to her presence. Or to direct the native man to her position, whatever it might be. Truly, she had no idea whether she walked closer to town or stumbled farther away. All she knew, that she escaped the precarious situation she'd found herself in, didn't ensure her safety.

Wylder. The only way out of peril, to find the damn town. There should be safety in numbers—even if the outlaws and bandits were rough, they had to be better than this isolation. And much more desirable than struggling through the dark.

Pansy heaved to her feet. Her shin smarted, and it felt as if every muscle in her body had been pummeled, but she forced herself to move. The more space she could put between herself and the man who, hopefully, still slept beside the campfire, the better.

The minute she heard the soft snores coming from his side of the fire, she fled. It had crossed her mind to give him a whack on the head with a stone, just to keep him slumbering, but when she grabbed a rock and crept close, she couldn't do it. If he hadn't been kind to her, she would have smacked him without remorse, but he hadn't harmed her in any way, and that had to count for something.

She chanced a look over her shoulder. Darkness, so complete she could have her eyes closed and not know the difference. As soon as she'd cleared the circle of cottonwoods, the fire's glow vanished. A look above showed stars glistening in the sky, but they were of no use to her. Father had never taught his daughters about constellations or positioning according to the night sky, so while they looked lovely, they certainly were no help at all.

A small circle, to get her bearings. In the distance, faint outlines that didn't look like part of the landscape. And every now and again, sound carried on the night air. Snatches of laughter and hoofbeats. Once, what sounded like a gunshot.

She pressed on, shifting her bag from one hand to the other. Her arms felt stretched, still from being tied behind her back around the base of a tree, and the bag grew heavier with each step, but she did not leave it. Who could tell what had become of her trunk, after it had been left beside the rutted trail. The only possessions that stood between her and abject poverty were in her bag, and she meant to bring it to town even if it cost her every last ounce of strength.

She had no idea where she'd go when she reached Wylder.

Most would go to kin, but she had no intention of letting her sisters take control of her life again. No, she'd come too far and endured too much to allow that.

Whatever happened, she would make her own way.

The plan, to avoid Wylder and head farther west, did not seem imminently feasible. Until she found out when the next Union Pacific pulled into—then out of—town, she'd have to lie low and avoid detection.

But where?

Well, she would figure that out when she got there. For now, one foot in front of the other.

Part of her—a big part—wished she hadn't left Clive Cooper's company. In their short acquaintance, the man had left a mark on her mind and heart. Something about him touched her in a way she'd never experienced before.

The way he quirked the edge of one lip up when something amused him. His knowledge of the terrain and the quiet conversations they'd shared about wildlife, mountains, trees, and even flowers. He had traveled extensively and, without being a braggart or condescending, shared the experiences. And that he did it all with her, a stranger he'd offered a safe seat on a train, touched her heart. The man had been kind to her from the very instant they met.

And that kiss. She had no idea another person's lips could be so divine or make her feel the way his had. Those moments when they kissed were some of the best of her entire life.

Heat warmed her chest, right in the center above her heart. She closed her eyes and let herself fall back in time, to the instant when she'd leaned forward and—

Another stone beneath her sole twisted her foot, and she stumbled. Her eyes flew open, and she managed to keep from falling, but just barely.

One foot in front of the other. This was not the time

to lose herself dreaming about a man who she would never see again.

Her breath hitched as she shifted her bag between hands. If the darn thing grew any heavier, she would have to take some of the items out and either leave them behind or stuff them down the front of her blouse.

Focus on getting to town.

Her mind drifted back to the stack of letters in her satchel. They were priceless, links to sisters and a family long gone from her. The missives had given her hope that somewhere in this western territory she would find a home, a place to settle and maybe even experience some happiness.

It had happened for the others. Why not her, too?

One letter from Violet stood out from the rest. Pansy had read it so many times the words were committed to memory. Now, she savored the tidings as she walked.

December 17, 1878

Dear Pansy,

Well, sister, it is nearly Christmas. How I wish you were here to experience Christmas in Wylder with me! There is no way to compare what goes on here with the festivities that you are experiencing in Charleston. There is less refinement here, and the rutted, icy streets look barbaric beside your beautiful cobblestone walkways and lanes. Still, the spirit of the holiday is in the air— even if that air often reeks of whiskey or cattle, depending on which of Wylder's roads you traverse.

Still, the people of this frontier town do put a lot of effort into observing the season. Neighbors visit in evenings, and the mercantile is a flurry of excitement. Children look longingly at sweets, and fruit is more abundant as Finn Wylder, the owner of the mercantile, orders a bit of extra for families to experience the treats of the season.

You would like it here, I think. While I miss home sometimes, it is a faraway longing rather than an intense, stabbing yearning. Don't get me wrong. When I first arrived here, I yearned. But now, I have settled in, and I do say have become one of the townspeople. No longer a newcomer, which is a gift, indeed.

Pansy, Wylder is—

Something hit her from behind, and Pansy fell to her knees, then onto her belly.

Fear flooded her, filling every cell in her body and turning the weariness that slowed her steps to fierce determination. Fight and live, the only real option that made sense.

She reared back, hoping to send her attacker from her back.

A mountain lion! I have been found by a hungry predator!

Strong hands on her upper arms grabbed her. They pinned her to the ground while the weight on her back pressed her ribs painfully against the satchel she still grasped.

Hands. Not paws.

The assault came from no animal, but a man! She thrashed from side to side, an attempt to dislodge the person who tackled her. Unsuccessful, as the one who lay upon her outweighed her by a good measure. Still, she could not lie still and be assaulted.

If she could reach the derringer in her pocket… But no, her arms were pinned too tightly to her sides. The best she could do, send an elbow back into the assailant's gut, brought some relief. The weight lifted, and the hands turned her. Roughly, not with care, she was slammed against the ground.

She whipped her head from side to side, hoping to send her forehead into the other's nose. A fine reward for the assault, to have a broken nose. And it would most likely force the man to release her. Then, she'd have time and space to go for her gun.

"Stop that!" The man hissed against her cheek, angling his face so her flailing could do no harm. "Lie still and be quiet. There's no telling who is out in this dark. Do you want to bring attention to yourself?"

The voice. She recognized it instantly.

A shiver went through her as he turned her over and pressed his body against hers. The first time she had ever felt a man on top of her brought shocking realizations. She hadn't imagined him to be quite this heavy. Or smell as strong and untamed. The scent of woodsmoke and pine trees swept up her nose, invaded her mind, and jumbled her thoughts.

She'd hoped to get away without seeing him again. Now the explanation he so clearly expected had flown from her head.

His face hovered above her, inches from her own. Even in the darkness she saw the flame burning in his eyes. She'd angered him, that was clear.

Mother's voice cut through the swirl that invaded her mind. *From the frying pan into the fire.*

Well, maybe so. But even a woman getting incinerated in a storm of her own making deserved a last breath.

Pansy pushed against his chest.

"I'm not letting you run off again." A line appeared between his eyes as he hissed, "Not until I know what you're doing."

She shoved his solid form a second time, his muscular chest a wall above her palms. "I'm trying to breathe." Another, none-too-gentle push. "You're squashing me!"

He raised himself onto his elbows but didn't remove his body from hers. Breathing came more easily…but the glare he shot her didn't shrink with the added distance. If anything, his gaze grew more penetrating.

While she refused to look away, she couldn't help but squirm beneath such scrutiny.

The man's brow rose. The whisper of a grin crossed his face. "You didn't have to lure me out into the darkness for that." He jerked his head back toward the inky darkness. "We would have been more comfortable near the fire."

It took a few heartbeats for Pansy to get his meaning, but when she did, her eyes rounded. Her wiggling—it had given him the idea that she… Good Lord! She had jumped into the fire and was about to burn for her stupidity!

"No! I didn't…that is, I don't…" She tried to swallow, but her mouth had gone bone dry. Probably affected by the fire rising around her, she thought. How to make this savage understand that he couldn't have his way with her? That she hadn't been encouraging him to…to…why, she couldn't even pull the words together in her own head! "No! Just no!"

Well Satan himself would be freezing before she would let this man—or any man—take her without a fight! She bucked on the unforgiving ground, dug her heels into the rocky soil, and heaved as hard as she could against him. The carpet bag fell from her fingers, so she curled them and brought her hand up between them, thinking to swipe his face with her nails.

The man caught her intention and grabbed her wrist, stopping her hand barely an inch from his skin.

"Whoa! There's no need for that." He rolled to the side, so she lay free of him, but kept a grip on her arm. "I do not intend to hurt you."

"You say that, but you kidnapped me!"

He shook his head. "I saved you from being sold."

"That's what you say." She tugged on her arm, but he held fast. "How do I know you're not lying? I don't even know your name, for God's sake!"

His fingers loosened on her wrist, not enough to release her but no longer tight. "I do not lie. My people, we leave that to the white man." His words were spoken softly, and his tone soothed her racing heart. "I speak the truth. I could not watch while you were sold, so I intervened. I planned to bring you to your people, your schoolhouse, come daybreak."

Her schoolhouse?

She remembered that she'd told him there were those who expected her, that she came to Wylder to be a schoolteacher. It impressed her that he had not forgotten.

She wanted to believe him.

"Why did you say what you said, then? About my, ah…" She should have kept her mouth shut, but now that she'd begun, she had to finish. A big swallow for courage. "What you said about the fire, staying by it instead of being out here…"

The tiny lip quirk returned. It seemed he enjoyed watching her embarrassment.

"I misspoke. I should never have said that." His gaze turned serious again. "My ancestors would not approve

122

of my behavior. I am sorry." He released her wrist, so she pushed herself to a seated position. He did the same. When they were eye to eye, he asked, "Why did you run? Don't you know you can get hurt out here?"

"I need to get to Wylder."

He waved a hand to the surrounding darkness. "This is an untamed land. You cannot expect the barren plains to be welcoming. There are many that would do a woman harm."

She tipped her chin up, a defiant act that came without thought. "How do I know you don't mean to do me harm?"

"If I wanted to harm you, I would have already done so." He looked away, into the darkness over her shoulder. Then he turned and met her gaze again. "I rescued you from those who would hurt you. I fed you from my own pot, the nourishment of my people. I offered you the treasured blanket made by my mother and gave you a place beside my fire."

His words stung. They were all true, and now, sitting on the unforgiving ground in the middle of the night, she felt ungrateful. And foolish.

"I'm sorry."

"I do not want your remorse. And my name is Hosa." He hesitated, then added, "In your language it would mean Little Raven."

Little Raven? This big, strong warrior certainly didn't look like any small bird, but she knew better than to mock him. Instead, she offered up her own fictitious name. "I'm Priscilla Buchanan." Mother's etiquette lessons brought what felt like a ridiculous statement, but she couldn't help herself. "Pleased to make your acquaintance." She swallowed when he didn't reply.

"And I really am sorry."

His gaze pinned her. "You run from me because I am not a white man. You fear what you do not know or understand, hurrying to get back to the people who brought you to this position." He shook his head. "If your white people had been as hospitable and compassionate as the savage you now sit with, you wouldn't be alone with me, would you?"

The enormity of the last few days crashed over her. She hadn't shed many tears when her parents died, or when she left her life behind, but they fell now. Hot and fast, followed by sobs that nearly tore her apart.

The man's expression gentled. He held a hand to her cheek, wiped away the tears with a calloused fingertip. "Don't cry. I did not mean to be so harsh." He scrubbed a hand over one cheek, then the other. "I only speak the truth, and that truth is something that brings me sorrow. How can our peoples, yours and mine, ever find peace if we don't learn to trust each other?"

Pansy had no good answer for him, so she kept her thoughts to herself. But she wondered if she would ever again find the peace he spoke of in this lifetime. While she told herself she planned on making her own decisions and forging her way in the world, she had never felt more alone than she did now.

****

Hosa walked Pansy to the railroad depot. He carried her valise, setting it down on the empty train platform. A tip of his head toward the closed office. "Your trunk is in there, Miss Buchanan. They will keep it for you until you claim it."

She looked from the wooden building to the man beside her. Both seemed shuttered and distant. "How did my luggage arrive in Wylder? The last I saw of it, it was thrown aside in the dirt beside the trail."

The man gave a huff of what she assumed was a cross between disbelief and annoyance. They hadn't spoken much as they walked the last of the distance to town, and now that they arrived, she could hardly expect him to linger, but it would be nice if they could at least part without these unnecessary—and impolite—noises.

"Remember, I did not put your belongings on the trail. I'm just the one who went for them and brought them here." He waved a hand toward the closed door. "I don't know when the stationman arrives, but he knows to expect you."

"How will he know it's me? You didn't even know my name until an hour ago."

He placed his hands on his hips and widened his stance. A few moments passed, then he admitted, "I said to expect a pretty white woman with golden hair."

Pansy smiled for the first time in longer than she could remember. Her hand went to her hair and smoothed it down. Certainly, she looked a mess. But his sentiment touched her heart and gentled her feelings a bit.

"Why, that's very kind of you."

He shrugged, pulling the vest he wore back and exposing the handle of the knife he wore at his hip. "I spoke the truth." His arm went up, and he pointed to the buildings visible from where they stood. Too early for most to be about, the place seemed nearly deserted. "The schoolhouse is over there. And Wylder Street is just that way." He nodded to spots beyond the train station. "The town is like most others that white men build. A main street with necessary shops, like a mercantile and dressmaker. Churches so your people can worship indoors. There are, ah, places for men to take their drink and find other diversions. I don't need to tell a lady to take care near those spots."

No, he didn't. Although while she knew she couldn't serve alcoholic beverages or dance in a saloon because it would draw attention to herself, both sounded intriguing.

Her best bet, to catch a train to the next western town, where no one would see her as part of the Bloom family. She wasn't ready to deal with any of her sisters, not yet. Maybe not ever.

"When does the next train come through?" She looked down the railroad tracks and saw a deserted lane. No sign of movement, not even among the brown scrub beside the tracks. "Do trains pass this way often?"

Hopefully Wylder was large enough that their service might be consistent. She didn't expect Chicago timetables, but there had to be something coming this way soon. Didn't there?

Hosa grinned. "It depends on what you consider 'often,' I suppose." He wiped a hand over his cheek and raised an eyebrow. "The next Union Pacific should be here early next week. Tuesday, if it's on time."

Tuesday. Next week? Oh, good heavens, but that wouldn't do. How on earth could she elude her sisters' notice for that long? Surely, they would spot her, even if she only left her boardinghouse room for meals. This place had a gossip chain that would have her secrets out before she could catch a breath. She knew that much from the letters her sisters had sent. They'd joked about the Wylder grapevine, but now that Pansy found herself a possible topic for the Nosey Nellies, she didn't find it at all amusing.

No time to waste. If she were to be stuck in this town for a week, she'd best find a place to hunker down. And take a bath. A nice, long one.

"Well, thank you, Hosa, for helping me the way you have." She tipped her head to the side and studied him for a long moment. "Although I have to admit, I'm still not sure I understand why you did it."

A sigh, so long it went on for several heartbeats. "I told you, it is not right for men to sell women. My people don't do that, and I can't watch it done without acting." He paused, then locked his gaze on hers. The dark eyes were wise, and the look serious. "I will become friends with the whites, but I will never bend toward their will. If we can live together in harmony, my ancestors will not be happy that we have been invaded, but they will be more at peace that we do not kill each other. So, I did it more for my people than you, if that makes sense."

Pansy nodded. "It makes a lot of sense. Thank you—and please, thank your ancestors for me, too."

****

The town still slept.

It didn't take long for Pansy to walk down Wylder Street, or to see that it would offer no concealment from discovery by her sisters. And she did want that, to have some time to herself to consider what her next move might be, without their constant chatter and well-meaning-but-overbearing declarations about what she should do with her life.

She might be off the mark from her original plan for this move, but she wasn't desperate enough to let the Bloom trio decide her mind for her. Not yet, anyway.

Her first thought, to spend a few days at the

boardinghouse, wouldn't do. Her assumption that the move would ignite a fire to the gossip chain was almost certainly a given. How on earth could she expect to stay so near to the center of activity, right in the heart of things, and not think she'd be caught out? She couldn't.

The hollow in her belly began to protest. A rumble, soft yet insistent, came from her gut. Last night's meal had been delicious, but it had been long hours and a lot of exertion crossing the dark frontier since she'd eaten.

The yeasty aroma of bread lured her toward a small bakery. The door stood open, so she peeked inside. Empty, save for the woman behind a wooden counter. The proprietress smiled and waved a hand, beckoning Pansy inside.

" 'Mornin'." The woman wiped a floury hand down the front of a white apron. Beneath the white expanse, a plainly made flowered dress, its sleeves rolled back to reveal an inch of the woman's wrists. It would have been scandalous in Charleston to show that skin, but here in the western heat, it appeared necessary. "What can I get for ya?"

A hard edge to the words, and an uneducated twang. Friendly, though. And what the speech lacked in finesse, the baked goods arranged in the glass-front display case made up for with their beauty. Soft, pillowy golden loaves of bread. Muffins, berries and nuts bursting from their domed tops. Cookies, so large and round they were the size of toddlers' heads.

She could have easily eaten her way through the lot, taking a bite from each, had her purse been heavier. Saliva pooled in her mouth as she surveyed her options. Finally, she pointed to a blueberry muffin.

"One of those, please." Her fingers found the coins

in her skirt pocket. She pulled one out and laid it on the countertop. When the muffin, still warm and wrapped in a square of brown paper, came her way, she took it with a grateful smile. "Thank you."

"My pleasure."

Just then, her belly gave a fresh growl. "Oh, pardon me!" A wave of heat flooded her face.

She needn't have been embarrassed. The other woman smiled and shook her head, exposing a missing front tooth. Now that she'd come close, Pansy saw the lines on the other's face, the gray hairs at her temples, and the sag at her cheeks. The woman's life hadn't been easy, and it was written on her face.

Still, the expression she offered was both kind and amused. She reached back into the display case, removed a cookie, wrapped it in brown paper, and placed it on the countertop. "Here. It sounds as if you need one of these, too."

When Pansy went for her pocket to get some more money, the woman shook her head.

"That's a gift, no need for coin." A tilt of her head to the side, and a penetrating stare. It only lasted a few seconds, but Pansy felt as if she'd been undressed and examined. "You ain't from around here, are ya?"

She took the cookie and gave a small smile as payment. "Thank you for this. It looks delicious." After she tucked the treat inside her pocket, she met the other's gaze. "No, I'm not."

"First time in Wylder?"

The woman was persistent. Ordinarily, Pansy admired persistence, but that didn't apply now. Not when her focus, on spending time in town undetected until she managed to find a way to Laramie or beyond, was paramount. She couldn't afford anyone, especially not a shop owner who most likely knew nearly everyone in town, to discover her secrets.

But the lady waited for her reply, so Pansy nodded. "Yes. First time."

And last, she thought.

"Well, we're mighty happy to have ya here. Whereabouts are ya stayin'?"

Good Lord, but the woman could be a U.S. Marshal with these probing questions!

Pansy wracked her mind for a way to leave without being offensive. She knew that if she left a bad impression with the shopkeeper, especially after she'd so kindly given her a free cookie, she'd be remembered. One tended not to forget those who leave a bad impression.

Lady Luck finally found her, though. As she opened her mouth, not quite sure what would come out, two cowboys entered the shop. Dirty, reeking of cattle and body odor, with spurs that jangled with each step they took, the pair grabbed both women's attention.

They turned toward the doorway to watch the men come in.

A chance to exit, one that might not come again. Pansy turned back to the other woman, gave a small smile and an even tinier nod, and stepped away from the counter.

"Thank you!" The words came out a bit nasal sounding, as she held her breath while passing the men. Their stench made her eyes water.

"Come on back anytime, ya hear?" The men had begun their order, so the words were nearly lost to the male rumblings, but Pansy waved a hand over her shoulder and made for the door. Not the politest exit, but it would have to do.

Outdoors, she paused to gulp in a breath of fresh air. Heavens, but didn't men realize how distasteful they were, shrouded in foul odors like that? Apparently not, she decided. Or maybe they simply didn't care who they offended.

She took a few steps from the shop. Her heart softened. Perhaps they were tired and hungry, and thought to not meet up with anyone while they procured their breakfast. Sure, that made sense. Still, she'd never met such offensively smelling men before.

Father had smelled like Bay Rum. Filly, printer's ink and old books.

Hosa had a wild, untamed scent. Being near him reminded her of standing beneath a pine tree. She hadn't minded it one bit—except when he'd been tying her to a tree. Then, she would've done anything to get away from him, despite the pleasing natural odor of the man.

She reached two fingers into the paper-wrapped cookie bundle and snapped off an edge of the buttery treat. She pulled it out and stuck it in her mouth, chewing as she walked.

Her mind wandered, back to the hours on the train in the company of the man who hadn't been far from her thoughts. Not since she'd met him, and certainly not since she'd left the train without saying goodbye to him.

Clive Cooper. The man's chiseled features and heart-fluttering grin made him easy on the eyes. And the scent of him, all musk and spice, turned her knees to jelly. She closed her eyes, allowing the memory of the feel of his lips pressed against hers to invade her head. Probably the best recollection of her lifetime, those precious moments they'd shared.

Her toe bumped something hard, so she opened her eyes and looked down to the wooden walkway. A stone, deep red and nearly as big as her palm. She bent down and picked it up, bringing it close so she might examine it. Not man-made, but natural, a rock or mineral she had never seen before. Certainly nothing like this existed in South Carolina, not that she knew, anyway.

"You have found some red jasper." A man's voice startled her, so she tore her gaze from the chunk of stone in her hand.

The man before her wore a vivid blue shirt with elegant silver swirls woven into the fabric. His skin, the loveliest shade of olive, and eyes a dark brown. His hair, shining black and sleek as an otter's fur, hung in a long braid down his back. His smile lit the day, brighter than the sun and just as warm.

He's Chinese.

She remembered her sisters writing about Lin, the Chinese woman who Violet discovered hiding in a cupboard of her schoolroom. The woman now lived with Violet and had practically become a sister to them from the sound of their letters.

Her gaze swept over the storefront behind him. A sign hung beside an open door. Wei's Gemstones. She glanced beyond the doorway, hoping her sisters' friend was not with him. Fortunately, the shop stood empty.

"Ah, hello." The first time she had encountered a Chinese person. Did she assume he spoke English or were the few words he'd offered the extent of his language skills? No way of knowing, so she pressed on. "It is jasper, you say?"

A nod. He reached his hand out, so she placed it in

his palm. With a smile, he held it up to the sunlight.

"Yes, jasper. Red jasper, to be exact." He turned it in his fingertips, and she saw streaks of brown, black, and gold beneath the dust on the surface. "A very nice specimen. Probably dropped by someone passing by. See the colors? They are minerals and impurities that are found in the stone."

"Impurities that make it so pretty? I've never heard of such a thing." Imagine that. The jasper's irregularities showed up so beautifully, as if they were intentionally painted on the stone to enhance its appeal.

He held the stone in his palm, rubbing a fingertip over its surface. "Oh, yes. Many times in life, the imperfections are what show true character, bring out the unique nature of a being. Or in this case, a stone." He grinned, his eyes lighting up as he warmed to the subject. "But remember, so-called perfection is an illusion. We are all imperfect, with our own individual brilliances that make us who—or what—we are. If you have a moment, I will be right back."

Without giving her a chance to reply, the man turned and went inside his shop. She peered in, but the shades were still drawn over the windows, and she could not see much. Just that the place had been empty. And now that he stood behind a table, bent over and rubbing the stone in his hand.

It crossed her mind to leave. Townspeople had begun to show up on the walkways that ran in front of the storefronts. Wagons rattled on rutted streets. Dust rose from the hooves of a rider's horse as he headed toward the mercantile. The longer she stood out in plain sight, the greater the chance she'd be recognized as a Bloom sister.

But if she left without giving the man a proper goodbye, he would remember her. Again, the idea she might not be easily forgotten kept her from moving.

He appeared almost as quickly as he left and held his hand out to her. On his palm, a stone that bore little resemblance to the dusty hunk she'd found. Polished so its colorful veins showed clearly, the jasper had been transformed.

Pansy took it from him. "Why, you worked some magic on the ugly rock I found! Thank you so much."

"My pleasure." He folded his hands at his waist, laying them over his slender midsection. "Jasper has many properties that are beneficial. It is a fortuitous event, to find such a thing. It was meant for you to find it, certainly."

"What sort of properties?" This mumbo-jumbo over a stone seemed silly, but the man's countenance showed he did not tease. And, with his hands folded so serenely, he appeared full of wisdom. Suddenly she found her interest piqued—and over a stone, no less.

Wonders of the west. They're just jumping up to greet me, it seems.

"Jasper is considered a very powerful healing stone. It is used for protection. For balancing energy, allowing for peace and prosperity." He hesitated, and his lips twitched. A shrug as he added, "It is also known to increase fertility. So, with a stone such as the one you hold in your hand, many things are coming your way."

At a loss for words, she nodded. "Thank you."

"Of course." He tipped his chin toward his chest and offered a small wave as she walked away.

Protection. Peace. Prosperity. She'd welcome those. But fertility? No, thanks. She had enough trouble finding her own way in the world. She couldn't imagine caring for a child, too!

****

The townspeople of Wylder didn't let any grass grow beneath their feet, not when it came to rising in the morning and getting on with the day. Pansy suspected that held true for everything else, also.

Life in the Wyoming territory, what little she had seen of it so far, showed itself to be drastically different from the carefree, relaxed lifestyle of the deep south that she knew so well. This place, with its underlying sense of danger and jagged appearance, had already taught her to move quickly and carefully. How much deeper did those instincts go with those who had been here a while? Much deeper, she imagined.

Now, wagons rumbled over rutted lanes. Foot traffic on Wylder Street picked up, with folks headed to do their morning shopping. Merchants, smiling at passersby, opening shops and setting out display tables on the walkway. A line of horses, their reins draped over a wooden rail, stood in front of the small diner. They waited, shifting weight and swishing their tails to chase flies as their owners ate.

All friendlier than she thought it would be. No sign of drunkenness or imminent danger, but that didn't put her mind at ease. As long as she had nowhere to go, no place to hide from her family while she contemplated her next move, her vulnerability to discovery made her heart race. At her right temple, a pulse beat an incessant tempo, a reminder that she wasn't safe, not even in the friendliness of a Wylder morning.

The railroad tracks. She had gotten a glimpse of a settlement of sorts just beyond the tracks, headed out of town. It looked like mostly women and children beneath makeshift tents. Perhaps she could find shelter there, hidden in plain sight among others who had lost their way.

She headed toward the train depot. Hosa promised her trunk would be there when she called for it. While she couldn't take possession now, she could at least peek into the depot and maybe spot it in a corner someplace. It would settle her nerves, to see that familiar trunk.

Pansy stayed close to the buildings, on the shadowed side of the street, with her gaze lowered. Not meeting anyone's gaze would save her from idle chitchat. Lord knew, engaging with any nosybody in town would have gossip flying, and she sure didn't want that.

No, she had to find a place to hide until the next Union Pacific train came through town. Or until she figured out what her next move would be.

Clearly, if she were to stay in Wylder for any extended period, she would have to make her presence known to Violet, Lily, and Daisy. But with that would come explanations about their parents' deaths, and she wasn't up to facing that. Not yet. Besides, her sisters would have so many opinions about her future once they saw her, and she was even less prepared to deal with any of that.

So, a spot to lie low. She'd love to find employment, but how could she do that without running the risk of being found out? She couldn't. No, the railroad encampment would be her best option.

Clive Cooper.

The memory of the man—or, more specifically, a wayward thought about how his lips felt pressed against her own—invaded her mind. Gooseflesh broke out across her forearms, and a shiver ran up her spine, as if just thinking of their wild moment had enough power to affect her body. Lord only knew where the man had gone. Surely, she would never see him again, but at least she had the memory of their kiss to hold on to. It would sustain her for a lifetime, or until she found another who kissed the way he did.

She didn't believe that would ever happen, that a man could make her feel as if they were the only two on the planet and that nothing else mattered. He'd melted her insides, stolen the breath from her lungs, and left his mark on her.

If she never met another who came close to making her feel the way he had, she would at least know that what she'd had with Finley didn't come close to being the best a man could offer a woman. She had thought there should be more but had no way of knowing. Until now.

With her gaze on the dusty ground in front of her and her thoughts miles away, she didn't see the woman coming toward her until they bumped into each other. Or, more to the point, she hit the large basket the woman carried and sent it to the ground.

The basket's contents scattered at their feet.

"What in tarnation?" The voice came out in a thin howl as its owner dropped to her knees. Black hair, held back by a cotton wrap, swirled around thin shoulders. "Don't you look where you're goin'?"

Pansy knelt beside the other woman and reached a hand toward the basket. It still lay tipped on its side, so she righted it and began gathering up the items that had fallen. A half-dozen apples, now covered with red dirt. She wiped them on her skirt before dropping them over the wicker edge. Oranges, too, so she scrambled to gather and wipe them.

"I'm so sorry. As you can tell, I wasn't looking and certainly didn't see you." She placed the last piece of fruit in the basket and met the woman's gaze. "It's my fault that this happened. I should have been paying attention."

A second basket, nearly as big as the one that had fallen, sat beside the woman. Now, the stranger sat back on her heels and wiped a hand over her forehead. Her face, flushed from the exertion of carrying two heavy baskets, had a hard edge to it. Her eyes, deep and dark, and with the glare of one accustomed to not being seen.

"Well, can't say as I haven't had my share of woolgathering moments." A sigh that sent an errant lock dancing beside her cheekbone. "We all have 'em, don't we? Moments when we wish we were anyplace but where we were, imaginin' ourselves walkin' on streets of gold."

Pansy offered a tiny smile. "I must admit, I was thinking of a place far from here, but the streets weren't even in my head." She reached for a bag of Arbuckle's coffee and set it into the basket beside the fruit. "More of a who than a where, is what kept my head in the clouds."

A knowing nod. "A man, then?"

"What else?" No embarrassment over admitting it to the woman, especially when her admission brought a knowing nod of sympathy. "I had my mind made up when I left home. No men until I settled in. My experience with them hadn't been good, and I thought surely I could do better on my own, without a man." She stretched her arm, reaching for a stray orange that had rolled close to the outside wall of the building they knelt near. It joined the others in the basket. "But here I am, daydreaming about a man I'll never see again, stuck in a place I didn't mean to be, and—" She met the woman's eyes and shrugged. "—knocking people's belongings into the dirt because I'm so caught up with the past that I'm not paying attention in the present." She glanced around. "I think we've gotten all of your supplies. Again, I'm so sorry for my clumsiness."

They rose to their feet, each wiping a hand down the back of their skirt. No telling how much dust they'd picked up in the time they'd been chasing runaway foodstuffs. Pansy took hold of the handles on her valise. It had been a welcome relief to set it down. Now it felt heavier than ever. How long could she wander the streets clutching the bag without falling on her face?

The other woman tipped her chin toward the bag. "Goin' somewhere?"

Pansy shook her head. "No." She hesitated, but it had been too long since she'd had another woman to confide in. "Just arriving, actually."

"Got kin in Wylder, have you? They must be waitin' on you." She raised an eyebrow. "Do yer need directions, then? To their place? I know most of the townsfolk…leastways, I know of 'em."

"No, no one's waiting for me." She swallowed, wishing for a glass of water. Between the heat and frontier grit, her throat had gone sore. "I just need to find a place to stay. Not forever, but for now."

The woman cast a shrewd eye over Pansy's form. Her gaze dropped to her toes, then back up to meet her eyes. The whole maneuver took less time than it took to blink, but it gave her the impression she'd been taken stock of. Did she pass muster? No way of knowing, was there?

"Not plannin' to stay in Wylder, then?" A calculated tone colored the words. "Just passin' through?"

Was she? Hard to tell, but for now, at least, she figured Wylder to be a temporary stop. Maybe that would change, but she didn't see how.

"I think so."

Another probing look, then the woman tipped her head toward the other side of the street. "Well, if you're lookin' for a place to stay, I can do ya better'n the boardinghouse can. If you're willin' to pitch in with the household chores, I can offer a room for no charge."

"Oh, no, I couldn't. Why, you don't even know me…I'm a stranger off the street, you can't take me into your home. What will your family think?" Pansy hated protesting, but she couldn't simply accept the kindness of this woman. The thought of a clean bed and a peaceful place to lay her head did appeal, though.

"We were all strangers once, until we became friends with each other." The woman lifted the heavy basket and balanced it in the crook of an elbow. "Besides, there's only me and my daughter. We've room to spare, and you sure look like you could do with some rest."

Her only other options, to either stay at the boardinghouse or hotel and be found out by her sisters, or find a spot in the encampment near the railroad tracks for the week she'd be stranded, paled by comparison to this one.

When opportunity knocks, open the door. Mother's words echoed in Pansy's head. She smiled as she gave the woman a nod.

"I'd like that, thank you."

When her new friend took off at a fast pace and crossed the street, she followed. It took a moment to catch up, the other moved so quickly.

They passed the schoolhouse and the schoolyard. Both were quiet, but the front door to the white building stood open, so she surmised her sister was already inside. For an instant she considered walking up the front steps and into the schoolhouse, but quickly shoved the idea aside. Violet would, no doubt, be happy to see her—but she'd also probably be full of notions about how her youngest sister should live her life. Pansy wasn't having any of it, so she kept her gaze on the road ahead and made her feet move beyond the schoolyard.

It hit her that she didn't know the other's name, so she turned and gave a small smile. "We haven't been introduced."

A snort, very unladylike and taking her completely by surprise came as her initial response.

Then the woman grinned, showing a mouth in need of serious attention. Wasn't there a barber in town? Back home, the dentist and barber did business in two separate buildings, but she'd heard that in the west one man generally took care of whisker cutting, hair snipping, and tooth extractions.

"Well, it's like this. My mama, God rest her soul, had big plans for me, but they didn't pan out like she thought they ought'a. No, instead of a life befitting the name she stuck on me, I came to much, ah, less hoity-toity circumstances." She nudged Pansy's side with one bony elbow. "No, I didn't end up in a fancy life, the way she planned. But the good news is she ain't around no more to see what's become of me."

Maybe she had jumped too quickly at this lodging

offer. They were off the main streets, winding through the lane of houses beyond the center of town. Back here, there wasn't anything fancy about the structures. Some were painted, while others were not. No wide walkways led to oversized doors. Porches were small, if there at all, and did not have pots of cascading flowers trailing over their railings.

She definitely wasn't in South Carolina anymore. And she didn't appear to be in the swankiest part of Wylder, either. But at least she wouldn't be hunkering down beneath a tree beside the railroad tracks. Whatever this woman's house lacked, it had to be better than sheltering beside a cottonwood.

Lord knew, she'd just had a night of that, and it had been no picnic. Her aching back could attest to the hardness of Wyoming soil.

"Mothers' dreams don't come true for a lot of us." She thought of her own mother. Had she not been in her grave, this adventure her youngest daughter had undertaken might have put her there. This way, with her gone, Pansy didn't have to regret one of her choices— not even the ones that were, like this one, showing themselves to be less than brilliant.

It would only be for a week, she reminded herself. She could do anything for seven days.

"Yer right 'bout that. My mama had big dreams, but her gal here got herself into some small-minded men's business." She turned and shrugged, as if that explained everything. "And yer know, once that happens, ain't hardly no way fer a woman to get herself untangled."

They stopped beside a modest structure. It wasn't as neglected looking as some of the others, which gave her hope. A two-story building, with a small porch. Painted gray, with white trim on the windows. A straight-backed wooden chair sat beside the front door, a book on its seat. Too far to see the spine and learn the title, the book gave her more hope that she had found a good spot to rest.

"Well, ya asked 'bout my name. I'm Cassandra, but most folks call me Sandy." She nodded to the house. "And this here's my place."

Pansy gave an appreciative smile. "You have a lovely home, Sandy."

"Aw, thank ya for that. It's not much, but it's mine." She cocked her head to the side. "And I don't think I caught your name, did I?"

No, she hadn't offered it.

A moment of indecision, then she went with the lie. "Priscilla Buchanan. Pleased to meet you, Sandy."

"Same here. People call you anything else? Priscilla's a mighty big name for such a mite of a woman."

Another moment of consideration. Mother had given in to Father's notion to name their daughters after flowers, and with the same middle name, to boot. All her life she'd thought it silly and would've liked a proper name. Now that she'd finally gotten one, she wouldn't give it up.

A firm shake of her head sent her hairpins slipping. "No, no other name. I'm called Priscilla."

"Well, then, that'll do." She took a step toward the front porch. "C'mon in, Priscilla, and meet my gal." When they reached the door, she placed her basket on the porch and put a hand on the door latch. "She ain't got a fancy name like you 'n me, but she's a good girl. C'mon, I think you'll like my Bess."

Chapter 8

Life within the tidy walls of the Wayans household had a routine to it that Pansy adapted to quickly. Cassandra made no bones about it, she expected her boarder to earn her keep, and that meant adhering to the schedule set forth.

Pansy roused herself before sunrise, went downstairs, and began breakfast. Arbuckle's coffee and toast, good for the constitution in her hostess' eyes. No deviation from the menu. By the third morning, Pansy would have given her best bonnet for a fried egg. But no, food didn't come cheap according to the woman in whose home she sheltered. Even when she offered to buy groceries, she was turned down. Besides being costly, excess food consumption made a woman plump, and Cassandra didn't take with round women. She made that abundantly clear.

So, breakfast, meager as if they were church mice scrounging a freshly swept floor, followed by household chores comprised the morning's activities. The place didn't require much to keep it clean. A sweep and scrub, as Bess put it. The inside of the simple home sparkled. Another thing the woman of the house loathed, untidiness. Pansy suspected dust didn't dare pass through the front door.

Fortunately, Bess proved to be a pleasant presence in the household. As different from her mother as a cactus from a flower, the young woman's smile and bubbly disposition made fast work of the chores. From what Pansy gathered, until she showed up, the household responsibilities fell squarely on Bess' shoulders. Her mother decided what should be done, and she did it.

"I'm so grateful you're here to help with things." Bess handed a heavy white cup to Pansy for drying as she dipped her fingers into the sudsy dishpan to retrieve the next one. The dinnerware, like so much else in the place, reflected Cassandra's no-nonsense outlook. There were no decorated plates or pretty teacups, only serviceable, plain dinnerware. "What a turn of good luck that Ma found you on the street that way."

A turn of luck, indeed, for all of them.

"I'm grateful to be here. Your mother is a kind woman, to take in a stranger the way she did." She dried the cup and placed it on the kitchen shelf. A nudge with a fingertip set the cup in alignment with the others stored beside it. The first time she'd dried the dishes and put them away, she'd made the ghastly error of not lining them up properly and had received a short, yet stern, lecture about it. The first lesson she learned by living with Cassandra and Bess? Everything must be in order to keep the lady of the house happy. Bess didn't seem to care one bit, but her mother had an entirely different attitude.

So, Pansy complied. It wasn't as if she planned to stay long, anyhow.

"Ma believes in taking people in. Showing them some hospitality." Bess lifted one slender shoulder, then let it fall. "Making folks feel at home is, ah, important."

Clad in a light blue dress that matched her eye color and offered a soft backdrop for the chestnut curls spilling down her back, she presented a picture of virtue. Pansy wasn't one to pass judgment, but she knew the truth didn't match the appearance.

The first night she'd been a guest, she went upstairs to the spare room early—at Cassandra's request. Tired and ready to consider her circumstances, as well as her plan for the near future, she went willingly.

Shortly after she'd gone upstairs, she heard bootheels on the back porch. Hard to miss the sounds, with the bedroom window open. Impossible to miss the ones emanating from the room directly below hers, either.

At first she thought Cassandra entertained a man, but the lilting murmurings gave Bess away. That night, three men came to call. Each night since, three or four clomped up, then down, the back steps and into Bess' room.

So she understood Cassandra's view on offering hospitality to strange men, all right.

Since it wasn't her place to judge what others did in their own homes, she kept her mouth shut and acted as if she had no idea the women were paying their bills by having Bess lie on her back and service men.

The western frontier didn't look kindly upon women on their own, and many found similar means to get by. Everyone knew that, including Pansy. She wasn't so young and naïve to not realize the facts.

"Yes, you're right." She rubbed the last cup dry and placed it on the shelf before she offered Bess the towel to dry her hands. "We all need to feel important, at least for a while."

A big sigh sent the other woman's shoulders drooping. The first time since she'd arrived, Pansy saw a frown appear on Bess' pretty face. The bow-shaped lips that usually formed a smile set in a hard, thin line, and a furrow creased her forehead.

"What's wrong, Bess? You're usually so lighthearted." She tucked her hands in the pockets of her dress and considered her words. She had an idea what subdued the other but didn't want to pry. Last night, just before midnight there had been raised voices from the room where Bess entertained. And when the bootheels stomped off the porch, they nearly shook the whole house. "Is there anything you want to talk about? I'm a good listener."

Her new friend folded her arms over her middle and dropped her gaze to the wooden floorboards. Her lower lip went between her teeth, and she took a deep breath, almost as if deciding whether or not to confide.

When her gaze met Pansy's, there was no sign of joy in the sad eyes.

"I've been seeing a fella. You know, kind of serious like." She paused, her eyes filling with tears. "He wants to marry me, make a decent woman of me, you know?"

A nod to show her understanding. No need to dance around the facts. Also no reason to shame the woman by inquiring further.

"Well, last night Todd, that's his name, gave me a choice. I can keep on the way I am, or I can marry him." She brushed a palm across her cheek, wiping away the tears that fell. "I told him I'm not ready to do that, that I don't know if I'll ever be able to on account of Ma. I can't just leave her after all she's done for me."

Pansy put a hand on the other's shoulder and gave a gentle squeeze.

"Do you love Todd?"

"I do. Oh, but I really do love the man." She reached into her dress pocket and pulled out a white handkerchief. A pause to blow her nose, then she added, "I never thought I'd love any man, not after my pa left me the way he did. Thought they were all only good for one thing, you know." Her brows quirked upward. "The money they can give. It's what brings security."

Not trusting her voice, or knowing what to say, she nodded, hoping the other would just go on without her having to comment. A small nod, to bridge the gap, was the best she could do.

Bess continued. "Ma picked me up off that church doorstep and raised me as her own. Pa, the man she married before she found me, left before I got too attached to him. So, it's always been just us. She needs me, to, you know, get by."

So much made sense now. The way Cassandra insisted Pansy retire to her room early, the evenings without the three of them sitting in the front room reading, sewing, or talking, the sounds of footsteps that cut through the night air. The women had a plan in place to add to their circumstances. Without the silver her daughter brought in pleasuring men, Cassandra might not be able to keep her home running.

Pansy suspected something was going on in the household, but this still came as a bit of a surprise. Suspecting something was one thing, but having her suspicions so clearly confirmed was another. As the full meaning of the conversation settled in, she hid her shock with a nonchalant shrug. "It's good that your mother has your, ah, help."

"Sure is. Why, I don't know if I can ever leave here to go off with Todd. What would she do?"

As she wiped at a nonexistent spot on the already shining wooden tabletop, her mind moved in circles. What would she do, indeed? Cassandra's circumstances weren't so far afield from her own. Women without men didn't do well in the harsh frontier—unless they used their brains, the way these women were doing, and found a way around a challenge.

"I don't know." Pansy hated to admit that she didn't have any good ideas to offer. She met Bess' troubled gaze and saw the other's heart written in her eyes. A woman in love, held back by dedication for someone who'd raised her and treated her as her own. Such a sad state. "I wish I knew an answer for you so everyone could be happy and safe." She offered a small smile. "But I'll think about it. Sometimes a fresh pair of eyes can see things we don't see ourselves."

Bess' expression softened. "I'd be mighty grateful." She glanced over to the window. Dusk had claimed the daylight hours. "I'd best get ready. Seems nights come fast sometimes."

****

Mornings were quiet in the little house. Bess wasn't an early riser, but her mother did make a pot of Arbuckle's at daybreak. When Pansy came down to the kitchen, she had it to herself, so she lingered over her cup of coffee and watched the sun rise beyond the window above the kitchen sink. A little bit of quiet before she had to begin the morning toast.

A peaceful start to a day. No pressure. No one to answer to. No decisions to make. Just a smooth beginning, with the hope of finding within herself what she wanted to do with the rest of her life.

A tug of homesickness pulled her thoughts to her

sisters. Their parents. Charleston. She had lost so much it took her breath away. How to ever build a life from such a mess?

Her mind drifted. Dark eyes, handsome features, a voice that sent her guts trembling. Clive Cooper swept into her thoughts and sent everything and everyone else off. Lord, but the man made her forget her troubles!

A smile tugged her lips upward. It still rattled her that she'd been bold enough to kiss him. Not a peck, either, but a real kiss. One that came from deep within her and left a mark on her like none other.

A once-in-a-lifetime moment. That's all it could be. She would never see the man again, but his memory would stick with her always.

Not for the first time, she wondered if leaving the train so abruptly had been a mistake. Maybe the biggest mistake of her life, even. But there wasn't any way to turn back time and make a different decision. She'd run, and look where it landed her.

She glanced at her surroundings. For now, a comfortable, safe spot, but there had to be more. She couldn't stay here forever. Hopefully, the next decision would be better than the one that led her away from the man who now haunted her dreams.

With a sigh, Pansy took a last swallow of tepid coffee and considered her plans for the day. So far, she'd been able to remain indoors and avoid seeing anyone, but that would surely come to an end soon. The other two women would soon suspect her actions. She'd spent the past two days cleaning the small house, and now there was little more to do, aside from the daily chores.

The end of her self-imposed hiding in place came sooner than she thought.

As she stood to wash her coffee cup, Cassandra flew into the kitchen. For such a small woman, she created quite a stir. Impeccably groomed, with a determined set to her angular features and looking as if she could take on every drunken cowboy in town, she beelined it for Pansy. In her hand, a scrap of paper that she dropped onto the table.

"I need you to fetch supplies from the mercantile this mornin'. You'll wanna go 'afore it gets too hot. I left some money on the table 'aside the front door." She met Pansy's gaze and raised her eyebrows. "Mind ya bring me back my change."

The mercantile! One of the places she most wanted to avoid.

What were the odds that one of her sisters would get a glimpse of her in a place like that? Good, she supposed. More probable, that she'd run into one of them, if not in the mercantile itself, on Wylder Street.

No, she could not go to the mercantile.

"I don't think I can do that today." No explanation, just a refusal. Maybe it would work, she thought. She kept her gaze neutral and hoped her hostess would decide to run the errand herself.

"Why, a'course ya can! You've done scrubbed the place top to bottom and everywhere in between, and you've only been here a few days. No, gettin' out is food for a soul. The mercantile will do ya some good." She nodded, nearly striking her chest with her pointed chin. "Money's on the table. List is right there."

"But, Cassandra, I really don't think—"

The older woman turned on her heel and headed out of the kitchen. Beyond, she had a small sitting room where she spent hours reading each morning, so it wasn't a shock that she went that way.

"No need to think." She waved a hand over her shoulder and added, "I ain't thought one bit 'bout whether ya have a bed in my house, so I'm sure ya won't think much 'bout doin' me a good turn."

Pansy watched her disappear into the sitting room and close the door with a small thud.

Her mouth opened, then closed.

Well, it looked like she was going to the mercantile, whether she wanted to or not.

****

Clive hated being outfoxed by anyone, but especially by someone who had caught his fancy, the way Priscilla Buchanan had. Damn, but the woman had grabbed his heart without his even realizing it. The heart he'd worked so long to protect, the one he vowed never to open up to a woman again.

Well, vows be damned. She'd breeched his defenses faster than an outlaw bent on avoiding a necktie social.

When he went looking for her on the train, she had vanished. No one saw her leave, but he figured she'd gotten off in the early hours at the Cheyenne station. The only explanation for her disappearance, other than her jumping from the moving train and that certainly didn't seem like anything a sane woman would do.

And Priscilla? Her smile hadn't been the only thing to grab his attention. The woman had a brain in her head beneath all those luxurious golden curls and wasn't afraid to use it. Her talk about making decisions without help and the companionable conversations they'd shared about topics from streetcars to Melville's whale book, *Moby Dick*, showed just how much intelligence hid behind her sparkling emerald eyes.

Her behavior in Chicago impressed him, too. Another woman would have crumpled to the ground, wailing over her misfortune, but Priscilla Buchanan had stood firm. She'd been upset, anyone would be over losing possessions the way she had, but she didn't fold. A man had to respect that strength.

Not for the first time, he wondered what all the woman had been through that had turned her spine to steel. She was young but determined. She'd shown that more than once in their short time together.

He had hoped to deepen their acquaintance—that is, before she turned up missing.

He'd gone on to Laramie and taken care of his business. The last report of his career as a gun for hire. A death certificate issued from a grateful lawman in a town that would no longer be brutalized by a hateful outlaw. One more occasion when he'd stepped up to help when the usual methods of justice failed. And a final payment.

The years he'd hired out had been good to him, financially. He had a fair amount put aside, and more on deposit in a bank back in St. Louis. But sooner or later, he'd have to find honest employment.

But first, to choose a place to settle down. They were all the same to him, the frontier towns that dotted the western landscape. With no family and no ties to anyone, he could remain wherever he chose. Get a job. Build a life. That plan carried him through the past few years, and it still felt solid. But now that he'd met Miss Buchanan, there were new thoughts running through his head.

The horse he'd bought in Laramie needed very little handling. It had been trained well and gave him no trouble. Sizeable, standing a good seventeen hands high, it presented a formidable appearance, but beneath the large frame beat a soft heart. A gentle giant who showed from the first instant he would serve his owner well. Clive had yet to come up with a name for the horse. As he rode into Wylder, he leaned down and spoke beside the animal's ear.

"You need a name. I can't keep calling you 'horse,' for Pete's sake." He ran a hand along the sleek neck. "How about Goliath? You sure do have the size to carry a name like that." He waited, but his mount gave no indication he'd heard. "Okay, not Goliath. What about Butch? It's a solid name, a respectable one."

The only sign the animal heard came from a nicker, followed by a head toss that sent its black mane flying. Not a sure sign the horse liked either name, but the conversation passed the time and gave Clive something to think about.

He had decided to backtrack to Wylder, then to Cheyenne if he had to, with the hope of catching up with Priscilla. Women didn't vanish into thin air. She had to be somewhere along the train route, and he meant to find her. He'd tracked nefarious men for a living for the last few years. Finding one woman couldn't be that hard.

Wylder's residents must still be mostly in their homes. On the outskirts of town, ranchers and homesteaders rode the ranges already. He'd seen enough riders on horses silhouetted against the sunrise to know their working day had begun. But in town, things started a bit more slowly.

A few wagons rumbled along the rutted lanes. Here and there, a horse and rider. A few women on foot, carrying baskets or tugging children by the hand.

An older woman, clad in drab clothing but with a bright green shawl tied around her shoulders, drove a buckboard filled with children his way. Headed for the school, probably. The kids looked eager to be out of the back of the wagon, and he wondered if she'd brought them in from past the town itself.

"Ma'am." He touched the brim of his hat. She nodded in return. A little girl held up a hand and waved, so he gave her a smile.

Small-town life. The backbone of society, the kind of existence he wanted for himself. Maybe someday he'd have a little girl like the one in the wagon, going off to school with other children and enjoying a safe, happy childhood. That's what he wanted…a home, family…all of it. But first, a woman to build that home with him.

Wylder's layout took no time to discern. Like so many other towns he'd ridden through, it had a logic to it. The railroad tracks, with buildings just beyond it. They probably housed less fortunate families, coarser businesses like the casket builder and cemetery keeper, and maybe even a house of ill repute. Most western towns had all those things, although they generally didn't show up smack dab in the center of town.

No, he expected the main street would be lined with shops. A hotel. Maybe two, if the place got enough traffic. A boardinghouse, which he planned to check into as soon as he spotted it. A mercantile and some smaller businesses, like a dress shop or perhaps a jeweler. Miners would be looking for a place to have their gold and gemstones weighed, and bought, so there would be establishments for that, too. And a barber, another place he intended to frequent.

A jail, certainly. A lawyer, for those who landed

behind bars. And at least one saloon.

As he passed many of the buildings on his mental checklist, he grinned inwardly. Exactly as he thought. Wylder could be any frontier town in the Wyoming territory. They were all pretty much the same, weren't they?

Wylder Street had the most action. He guided his mount down the center of the street, noticing the wide wooden walkways fronting buildings and the few awnings offering shade. Nice touches. Not every town had those, so maybe this place did step above the usual, after all.

He stopped in front of the mercantile, a large two-story wooden building with wide glass front windows. Impressive, to have such a big place to shop in such a small town.

When he dismounted, he secured the reins to the post in front of the building and stood for a minute. Riding did a man's back no good, and his fairly screamed now. A stretch to straighten out, and a reminder that he couldn't abide sitting in the saddle for days on end anymore. If he'd had any thoughts of changing his mind about this new life course, which he didn't, the aching bones would have swayed him. No, he'd chosen well. Every man should know when to step away from what cost him and settle into what would, hopefully, enrich him.

He took the steps two at a time and wondered if Wylder might be the place for him to plant some roots.

****

Pansy hated that she'd been forced into venturing out when all she wanted was to hide in place. It would be a miracle if none of her sisters spotted her, an absolute marvel if she managed to get to the mercantile and back without being discovered.

She had tried, even as she headed out the front door of the modest house, to persuade Cassandra that she wasn't suited to shop in the unfamiliar town. Her protests fell on deaf ears.

Truthfully, she thought her hostess might be pushing her out so she and Bess could have a bit of private time. Pansy had caught the two whispering in the hallway twice. By the stubborn set to Bess' features and the displeasure flashing in Cassandra's eyes, their conversation was one she'd rather not hear. Still, she could have sat in the backyard or worked in the vegetable patch. Anything but march into town where she could be seen.

Since there wasn't a way around the task, she would make haste. The sooner she grabbed Cassandra's supplies, the sooner she would be safely out of the public eye.

So, she kept her head down and headed toward Wylder Street. A child called from a passing wagon, but she didn't look up. No, the little one most likely headed for the schoolhouse. She couldn't chance being recognized by one of Violet's pupils. Children were intuitive, and she wouldn't be surprised if one recognized her either by her face or mannerisms. After all, Mother had raised them all to be good southern ladies, and that must show to outsiders.

She scurried past a lawyer's office and another office. Both had their doors open to the day, but she didn't glance inside either. Violet kept company with a financier, but her sister Daisy had become involved with an attorney, Addison Merriweather. No sense in tempting fate by showing her face near any law office.

No, she would scoot into the mercantile, grab the items on Cassandra's list, then rush back to the house. And hope to heck she wasn't spotted.

She sucked in a breath and kept her feet moving as she thought about her sisters. She missed them, she truly did, but she couldn't chance seeing her siblings until she got her own feet under her. They were all grown up, with menfolk and lives of their own.

Lily had gotten married. Violet had a financier. Daisy, a lawyer. And she? What did she have? Nothing. And no one, that's what. Well, she'd hold off standing in their presence until she could show she'd done well for herself.

For a while, back on the Union Pacific, she fancied she might have met a man who could share the life she envisioned. That Clive Cooper, he had caught her eye…gooseflesh rose on her forearms. Just the thought of him brought a shiver.

Mother would say a goose is walking over my grave. Forget about silly notions and concentrate. Focus. Find your way!

Pansy wanted desperately to make her mother proud. Silly, she knew, to think a dead woman would know how she fared on earth, but that was the truth of it. She believed Mother could still see her somehow, and she planned to show that she could forge her own way in the world.

But that man…

She shook her head. The man wasn't anywhere near Wylder, and in a few days she wouldn't be, either. Best to forget him and follow her own advice. Time to concentrate.

The mercantile loomed directly ahead of her. A large building, with wide glass windows in its front wall, it reminded her of a shop back home. Of course, this one didn't have gingerbread trim or a blue-and-white striped awning, but it was sizable enough that she imagined it held just about anything a heart could desire. Well, almost anything.

An impressive black horse stood near the hitching post. The animal resembled one Father kept in his stables. Favored for his even temperament, the horse accompanied her father on nearly every trip about town. When her parents passed, she had sold the horses. A pang of longing touched her heart, bringing her to a stop beside the animal before her.

She reached out a hand and ran it over the horse's neck. Its ears flicked at her touch, but it stood still. It took every ounce of self-restraint for Pansy to keep herself from burying her face in its mane. How she wished she could turn back time and stand in Father's barn with his beloved horse.

"Why, Miss Buchanan!"

That voice.

"Why, I do believe you are the very last person I expected to see standing beside my horse this morning." The sound of his throat clearing brought back memories of their time together. "It must be my lucky day, after all."

Oh, good Lord, she knew that voice. How on earth could it be that the man who haunted her dreams, the one who still sent a shiver of delight dancing along her spine, stood behind her? After all these days, he should be miles from here. He'd been on that train when it chugged out of Cheyenne. How could he be here?

She took a moment to steady her breath before she turned to face him. Sure enough, Clive Cooper in the handsome, rugged flesh. He smiled, as if they'd only just parted.

Words eluded her. She stared, pressing her back alongside the solid form of the horse. Its flank sent heat through the thin cotton of her blouse, and the solid form kept her knees from buckling. She leaned against the animal and waited for her heart to stop pounding.

When she didn't speak, he removed his hat and held it loosely in one hand, while the fingers on his other hand swept his hair away from his temples. Her gaze pinned the fingers, as the memory of their touch on her skin flooded heat to parts of her that had no business heating.

"It sure is a nice surprise, finding you next to my horse this way." He chuckled, then put his hat back in place. "I didn't expect it." A pause. "But, really, who does ever expect to find a beautiful woman in congress with a big, black horse?"

A beautiful woman. The words echoed in her head.

Behind her, the horse shifted, almost as if he were informing her that keeping the conversation moving sat on her shoulders now. She squared those shoulders and met the man's gaze.

"Good morning, Mr. Cooper."

The half-smile that she'd come to look for when they spoke appeared. "Now, then, I think we might be a bit more familiar than that, don't you? I addressed you formally, as well…but it does feel contrived. And hearing the words, well, I almost turned to see if my father is nearby." His smile widened. "A real trick, that, seein' as he's been dead for many years. But enough about my father. Please, call me Clive, the way you did…ah, the way you did when we were last together."

The last time they'd seen each other, she had been in his arms, pressed against his body. They had been kissing each other as if both their lives depended on it. Her cheeks warmed when his smile grew still more. So, he remembered, too.

It wouldn't do to discuss the circumstances of their last meeting, so she scoured her mind for a safe—and quickly resolved—topic of polite conversation. Time would not still, even though she could have easily stood and stared at the man for a while. Every moment she spent in front of the mercantile increased her chances of being seen by one of her sisters. She had to end this meeting and return to Cassandra's house.

The horse shifted a second time, bumping her shoulder with the side of his head. A gentle tap, but one that caught her attention. She reached a hand around and placed it on the animal's neck. "This is your horse? Does he have a name?"

"He is mine. And no, he doesn't have a name yet. If he did, the man I bought him from didn't divulge it." He nodded toward the animal. "Actually, we were discussing names this morning. The horse and I, that is. But so far we haven't found anything we both like. Do you have any ideas?"

She turned and stared into the horse's dark eyes. Such a magnificent animal. So tall and regal. He needed a name, and not just any run-of-the-mill one, either. Such a fine specimen of horseflesh deserved something fitting.

As a child, her favorite horse in the stable belonged to Father. Massive, spirited, and prone to tossing any other rider off its back, the animal had a glimmer in its eyes, the way this one did. Surely, a sign from above, maybe telling her she wasn't as alone as she thought.

Father sent you, didn't he?

She didn't expect a reply. But when the horse dipped his head and nudged her shoulder again, she didn't need anything more.

"Black Jack." She turned to face Clive. His lips quirked up at the corners as he considered the name.

"Blackjack? Now, I wouldn't've figured you for a card player."

She shook her head. Time for dawdling had come and gone, but she had to settle this before running off. "Not blackjack. Black Jack—two words."

He stepped forward and reached out. His hand came so close the scent of woodsmoke from his jacket swept up her nostrils. She wondered if he'd slept rough, the way she had the night before coming to Wylder.

"Whaddaya think, boy? Black Jack suit you?" He patted the animal's neck and gave a nod. When he met her gaze, admiration shone in his eyes. "I've been trying to come up with a good name since I handed the cash over to his previous owner, but nothing seemed right. I guess we were just waitin' on your help. Much obliged, Miss Buchanan."

"It's the first time I've ever named anything. I feel like I should be thanking you." She turned to the horse and gave it a last pat. "And you, Black Jack."

Pansy moved away and placed her foot on the lowest step leading up to the mercantile. "I've got to run. It was nice seeing you again." Mother would be happy she'd minded her manners, but it took a lot of effort to put distance between herself and this man. The truth of it, that she wanted to lean in and stand as near as possible to him, made no sense. But so little had, since she'd lost her parents, that she didn't question her feelings. Still, Mother raised her to be polite, so she tipped her chin to her chest and climbed the wooden steps.

"Miss Buchanan?"

She stopped on the boardwalk and swiveled to face him. "Yes?"

"It was nice to see you, too. Would you be interested in maybe taking supper with me?" He pointed to the Wylder Hotel. At this time of day, its wide front walkway stood empty, no travelers going in or out the big wooden doors. "I'm staying in town for a while, and I'd surely like to spend some time with you. That is, if you're free."

In another time and place, she would have jumped at the invitation—of course, in a refined, ladylike manner. Mother would have been proud of her daughter's genteel acceptance, and the evening would have likely been one to remember. But this time and place, and her circumstances, did not allow for such frivolous actions. She couldn't accept him, as much as her heart screamed that she would love to spend time in his company.

No, it wouldn't work. Someone was bound to see her, and even if she didn't get caught by one of her sisters, she looked too much like them to hope the family resemblance wouldn't be picked up by someone.

"I'm sorry, but I can't." A nod to show she considered the conversation over, and a few steps toward the shop entrance.

"I'm sorry, too." His voice, so deep and rich, made her pause. She resisted the urge to turn back. "I should tell you that I don't give up easily. Not when it's something—or someone—that catches my fancy. And you, Miss Buchanan, have caught me up like no woman I've met in a long, long time."

What could she say? The feelings were so mutual, yet they could go nowhere.

Pansy put a suddenly shaky hand out and pushed the wide screen door open and stepped inside the mercantile. She refused to turn around and meet the man's eyes, because she knew her resolve might crumble to pieces, like an overdone pound cake. Her eyes took a moment to become accustomed to the building's dim interior, so she stood still before moving away from the door.

Finally, she chanced a glimpse out the wide front window.

Clive Cooper and Black Jack were gone.

Pansy's heart dropped to her feet as she sucked in a deep breath and told herself it was for the best. There couldn't be a future for her with the man, or in Wylder. If she were to find her own way and make her own decisions, she would need to put distance between those who considered her too young to live her own life. And that meant getting away from the other Bloom sisters. As much as she would have loved being near them, she couldn't abide being told what to think and do any longer. If they weren't so hellbent on controlling her, it might be different. But they were, so it wasn't, and that meant she couldn't stay.

Nothing could convince her to allow others to dictate the direction of her life any longer. Not even the desire to get to know that charming man on a more personal basis. No, not even that.

Chapter 9

Pansy reached into the wicker basket and pulled out a wet bundle. She shook the fabric, sending water drops flying, and gave it a good, hard snap. Then she hung the white muslin sheet over the laundry line hung between two maples in Cassandra's backyard. There were two laundry lines. Bess hung garments over the other one, while she attended to the bedding. Both lines were filling quickly.

Monday morning washing. Back home in Charleston, it had been the day Mother designated for laundry, too. While Pansy and her sisters rarely hung wet laundry, leaving that to the housekeeper, they were no strangers to folding and pressing. Although the wet fabric weighed more than she thought it should, the chore required muscles and stamina but left room for daydreaming.

And she'd been so lost in her own thoughts that Pansy didn't realize they were suddenly not alone.

"You shouldn't be here!" Bess' frantic exclamation alerted her, so Pansy leaned down and peered between the sheets.

Men's boots. Brown, scuffed toes, covered with red dust. The owner had walked into the yard. If he'd been on a horse, there wouldn't be a fine layer of dust coating his footwear. No, he'd been on the ground, and that gave him the opportunity to enter the yard undetected.

Until now.

"You're the one who shouldn't be here. You should be with me, in our own home, raisin' a family." The last words were slurred.

"We talked about this—"

"It ain't right! I love you, and you won't see how much I want you." A hitch in the man's voice tugged at Pansy's heartstrings. He sounded tortured. "It just ain't right, I tell ya…"

Bess' voice dropped to a hiss. "Go home, Todd. You're drunk."

The urge to push through the laundry was great, but Pansy wasn't sure she should intrude. The man mightn't appreciate it, and she could make the situation worse. Bess seemed to have him in hand. Maybe he would do as he was told and leave, peacefully and without embarrassing the woman he claimed to love.

Her hopes crunched beneath the toe of his dusty boot. The tender tone turned belligerent in a heartbeat.

"You are comin' with me—right now, no more talkin' on it, you are—"

"Get your hand off my—"

"You're mine, ya hear?"

Pansy reached into the pocket of her skirt with her right hand as she pushed aside the wet laundry with her left. She moved forward, the wet sheet she'd just hung slapping her in the back.

She pulled out the under-over derringer Father had given her when she turned sixteen. He'd gifted one to each of his daughters and schooled them on how to use their weapons. In this moment, she wished she held the bigger six-shooter she'd taken from the man on the train.

But that sat at the bottom of her traveling bag in the

guest bedroom in the house behind them, and the threat to her new friend's safety stood five feet away. She raised the pistol to her waist and pointed it at the man.

"Let her go." Relieved that her voice didn't wobble, she repeated the words for good measure. "I said, let her go."

Bess' suitor was easy on the eyes. His shirtsleeves barely hid the muscular form beneath the fabric, and his blue jean trousers were filled just as nicely. His shoulders and chest stretched the brown leather vest he wore tight across his upper body. And the face, all bronzed, as if he spent a lot of time outdoors. The eyes were deep blue, and he'd been looking tenderly at Bess, despite the nature of their conversation. His right hand grasped one of Bess' wrists, but the hold didn't seem painful, merely possessive.

Now the man's brows rose, and his forehead creased. A slow grin stole over his mouth. "Well, well…now isn't that cute?"

She wasn't sure if he meant her, the pistol, or the way she burst through the wet laundry, but it didn't matter. Her shoulders dropped, and her spine straightened. "I said, let Bess go. Now."

Bess held up her free hand, placing it in front of the man beside her. "No, please. Priscilla, he means no harm, don't hurt him."

"I don't want to hurt anybody. But you asked him to leave, and he needs to go." She locked her gaze on Todd's and did her best to look fierce. "Now."

He loosened his grip, his fingers turning and stroking the underside of the woman's wrist. He glanced down, and his face crumpled. "Aw, heck…I didn't mean to hurt no one. I just wanna take Bess here to be with me…"

Bess turned her hand so her fingers threaded through Todd's. She met Pansy's gaze and shrugged. "He wouldn't harm anyone. He's just…" Another shrug.

"In love." The words were slurred, but the sentiment behind them sent shivers up Pansy's spine. No man ever looked at her the way Todd did Bess. His feelings were written across his face, for the whole world to see.

The object of his affection turned to him, and the sentiment in her expression mirrored his. It was almost too intimate for Pansy to witness, but she resisted turning away. The man, somewhat inebriated and insisting her friend leave with him, couldn't be trusted. Not in his present state, anyway.

"And I love you, Todd." Bess waved her free hand toward the house behind them. "But I told you, Mama needs me here to help with the house. As long as she insists on staying here, I can't go with you. And she refuses to move to a smaller place, or in with my Aunt Myra. I'm stuck." She placed her hand on his cheek. "You need to start facing that, 'cause it's not gonna change. Also, you need to quit drinking so much. It's not gonna solve anything."

He raised a hand to his head and adjusted the brim of his hat. That, too, brown and dusty, making Pansy wonder if he hadn't slept rough. But whether he did or didn't wasn't her concern. Truthfully, she'd grown tired of the interruption to what had been a peaceful morning. Bess didn't need the man's shenanigans, and neither did she.

Her hand ached from holding the pistol aimed at Todd for so long, so she shifted from one foot to the other and motioned with the derringer. "And I still think the lady asked you to leave."

Todd released Bess then and met Pansy's gaze. The blue eyes were bloodshot, filled with sadness and, if she had it right, remorse. Unfortunate for a man to be so low, but it wasn't her concern. Not really. In a few days she'd be gone, probably.

"I jes' cain't leave 'er. Ya don't un-un-unnerstan…" He waved a shaky hand over the center of his chest. "I love 'er so much it hurts." A slap on his shirtfront brought a meaty sound. "Right here. Fer real, it is. This here hurt, it could kill a m-man."

Bess placed a hand over his where it lay on his chest. She leaned close, put her cheek against his shoulder, and sighed. "I feel the same, Todd. But I can't leave my mama high and dry. Until she agrees to move, I'm stuck." She rubbed a gentle fingertip across his knuckles. "And you need to leave before Priscilla's finger slips on the trigger."

The man squinted, sending an almost-sober glare to the pistol. Pansy had no idea what went on behind the bloodshot eyes, but he seemed to be weighing his options. She hoped he'd choose wisely. It would be a damn shame to have to shoot him.

Finally, Todd nodded. He turned and brushed a kiss across Bess' forehead. "I'll go, but I'll be back. Don't think for a minute this 'ere's sett-set—" He scrunched up his lips and gave a fast huff of annoyance. "It ain't over."

She watched him turn toward the alley that ran between Cassandra's house and the neighbor's place. He took a few steps and stumbled over his own feet. He looked ready to pitch forward but somehow managed to find his balance. A few staggering steps took him back the way he'd come, with as much quiet determination as he'd brought into the yard.

Bess shook her head. "The man is lettin' it eat him up inside, that we can't be together."

"It must feel nice to have someone love you the way he does." She tucked the pistol back into her skirt pocket and sighed. "I've never seen a man so passionate about claiming a woman. I don't think he'll give up until he figures out how the two of you can be together."

The other woman turned and cast a wistful glance over her shoulder, but the object of her affection had gone. "That's got me concerned...he's like a dog worrying a bone." She met Pansy's gaze, trepidation showing plainly in the wide eyes. "What if he don't give up till he wears the flesh off me? What then?"

****

Clive didn't have one ounce of regret for following Miss Priscilla Buchanan—if that was her real name, which he suspected it wasn't—back to what he assumed to be her place of residence. He thought it unlikely she owned the little house, but one could never tell. He'd seen so many strange things and met far too many unusual people to count anything out.

When he'd seen her out early the first day, he figured she'd probably show again the following day. It had been his experience that most people fell into some kind of routine. So he rose early, left the boardinghouse before anyone else stirred, and tucked himself into the space between two buildings directly opposite the Wylder Mercantile.

It only took an hour for her to show. She strode along the wide wooden walkway without looking left or right. Her eyes turned to the wood beneath her feet, her chin tucked tightly against her chest as if she fought stiff winds.

The woman hid something, that showed clearly. He'd spent too many years finagling the truth from some and uncovering lies of others to be taken in by her sweet countenance. Maybe it came as part of the prickliness he still felt over her jumping from the train without a backward glance his way, or perhaps it showed his true nature, but Clive didn't trust her. He admired her feistiness, marveled over her intelligence and beauty, but trust? Nope. Most of the details of the nature of her travel and her life didn't add up. On the surface, they told a story...but his gut warned him there were chapters missing from her tale. And while everyone deserved to keep some bits private—hell, he did it himself—there were too many gaping holes in the woman's story for him to disregard.

Besides, he wanted to know as much as possible about the woman. She piqued an interest in a way that he hadn't experienced before. Sure, his head had been turned a time or two by a pretty face or a swish of skirts. But nothing prepared him for this. A hunger to know her spurred him on, to the point of standing in the shadows hoping she would make an appearance.

He'd had time to consider what he'd do if she showed up. Now that she had, it took a supreme amount of self-control to carry out his plan to watch, then covertly follow her home. It would be so easy to walk across the street, catch her as she exited the mercantile, and offer to carry her packages home. No woman could refuse such an offer of assistance, could they? Especially when it came with an invitation to walk over to the diner for a slice of pie.

His toes curled inside his boots, wanting to cross to

the other side of the street. But knowing Priscilla, even as superficially as he did, he expected she would find a way to avoid his attention. No, best to wait and follow. The original plan had merit, even if it did lack the added attraction of pie—and watching that beautiful woman devour every bite.

He checked his pocket watch when she passed through the front door into the mercantile. The proprietor, Finn Wylder, seemed the chatty sort yesterday when he'd been in, so he figured it might take a few minutes for her to emerge. Well, he had time, so he leaned against the wall of the building on his right and waited.

Either she got caught up shopping or Finn set her to chatting, because a full fifteen minutes passed before Priscilla emerged. A tiny smile pulled her lips high on the corners, as if the shopping pleased her. But as soon as she stepped out onto the walkway, her lips went flat and she spun her head to the right, then the left, checking the street. He wondered what she hid from, but there wasn't time to mull it over. The woman took off at a brisk pace, so he stepped out onto the walkway and set off after her.

Even with her moving quickly, he kept up without trouble. Long legs and years of outdoor work made him capable of moving without overexertion. A few times, he had to slow his own pace for fear of overtaking her.

When she turned onto the street where the house she'd been staying in was, he sped up. If possible, he'd like to get a peek into the residence when she opened the front door. A good way to tell what sort of circumstances she lived in, as well as getting an overall feel for the living conditions.

The woman hadn't given so much as a whisper of a hint that she would be staying with friends or family in this town—or any town, for that matter. He surmised her present situation had been a lucky accident. She hadn't any money that he knew of, although he suspected she carried something of value in her clothing seams. Most women did, but in his experience most only carried enough to sustain them for a short time or help work their way out of an emergency. He didn't believe she would use whatever she hid to buy a house, even a small one like the one she even now headed toward.

No, she had to be staying with the home's owner. He didn't know much, but he recognized a woman under cover.

He went down the list of things he actually knew about Miss Priscilla Buchanan.

An assumed name.

A satchel filled with letters she cherished.

Parents in the hereafter.

A slip from a train before sunrise.

Residence in a home owned by someone she most likely just met.

And a kiss that had seared itself on his soul.

Yeah, he had to find out more about the woman. He hadn't come this far in life to let a sweet southern belle claim his heart, then drive him mad with wondering about the truth of her. No, he'd uncover her secrets…one way or another.

****

Pansy worked the embroidery needle without thinking. She had learned to stitch when she'd been very young, barely old enough to hold a needle. Her talent for creating beauty from colored threads on plain fabric bloomed quickly, and the activity became one of her favorite pastimes.

Now she allowed her mind to drift back to her childhood home, to memories of sitting in the front parlor with her mother and sisters. Most spent the hours talking over their needlework, making afternoons special times. Lily usually held a book rather than a hoop. The eldest sister could pin an updo with ease, but her talent began and ended with hairpins. The embroidery needle or sewing pins vexed her. Mother had given up on teaching her firstborn daughter how to embellish the ordinary and hoped her sisters would gift her with enough of their handiwork to fill her dowry chest.

Those hours were some of Pansy's fondest memories now. Had she known then that they were to be short-lived, she would have put down her embroidery and just savored every single moment. But she had no way of knowing seemingly endless afternoons spent in the circle of womanly domesticity were numbered. No one could have known. She wondered if her sisters missed those times, too. No way of knowing that, either.

A deep breath to pull her back to the present moment, and a glance down at the fabric in her hands. She had offered to embellish some tea towels for Bess. She'd finished the first, and this one looked nearly complete. A spray of springtime flowers across the bottom, with leaves, tendrils, and vines climbing up the sides. Bess had protested that she didn't need fancy towels, but when Pansy learned they were being tucked away for the other woman's eventual home, she had to turn functional into pretty, too. This western life offered few splurges to women. The least she could do was provide a splash of beauty to Bess' future kitchen.

She looked up from the tea towel. Bess had taken down most of the washing hanging on the lines, but a few pieces remained. They hung in the late afternoon warmth, looking forgotten and forlorn. Left behind by their clean companions, to wait for their fate.

Pansy sympathized with the bedsheet and towels. She waited on her fate, too. Sure, she had the chance to make her own decisions now, but what of it? The prospect had seemed fabulous when she started out from home, but crossing through cities, past small towns, and into the wilderness had shown that her idea of plotting her own course and the reality of that were two different things. She'd thought to be beset with choices—exciting, wonderful, adventurous options—yet that hadn't happened. Deciding which muffin to eat for breakfast in the dining car or choosing which blouse to press wasn't much different from what she had done before.

It took her traveling west to realize life didn't offer huge decision options on a daily basis. No one had really been dictating the direction of her life. She had been too young, immature, and inexperienced to realize the truth.

A sigh escaped her lips. Last night, just before she'd closed her eyes and drifted off to sleep, she considered the possibility that she might be wise to go to Violet's house. It would come with a bit of embarrassment, and maybe some hurt feelings, because she would have to confess that she'd been hiding in Wylder. The sisters might even be angry with her that she'd chosen to conceal her presence from them. And truthfully, she wouldn't blame them if they were upset. She imagined she would be, in their shoes.

At the swish of the back door opening, she turned. Bess emerged, holding two mugs.

"I thought we might need a break." She handed a mug to Pansy, who inhaled the steam coming from the hot liquid. The scents were new to her and seemed fresh and inviting. "It's not as fancy as the tea I'm sure you're used to drinking, and Mama doesn't have any pretty teapots or cups, but it's good and hot and will give us a chance to sit a spell."

Pansy sipped the tea, loving the way the Earl Grey slid down her throat. The hot breezes that blew off the plains kept her feeling parched, so this came as a welcome surprise. She balanced the mug on the edge of the wooden bench while the other woman settled herself on the empty space beside her.

"I don't need porcelain teapots or tiny cups and saucers. This is wonderful, thank you." When Bess smiled, she placed the tea towel on the other's lap. "And your timing is perfect. I just finished this one. Now you can add it to your marriage chest."

Bess ran a loving fingertip across the sea of pansies, hyacinths, and daisies. A long moment passed as she studied the handiwork. When she looked up, there were tears in her eyes.

"It's so beautiful. I'm not sure I deserve anything this nice."

Pansy brought her eyebrows close and met the other woman's gaze. "Whatever do you mean? Of course you deserve pretty things. We all do!"

Bess dropped her gaze. She sucked in a deep breath and swallowed hard, before she spoke. "I'm not a lady, like you, Pansy. You haven't told much about yourself, but it don't take words to figure out some things. You come from good people and are better class than me and Mama." When Pansy opened her mouth to interrupt, her friend held up a hand between them. "No, no need for denyin' it. I'm not envious. I'm just stating the truth, and there's no need to say it ain't so. You come from a good family and are probably used to certain things that I've never known and, let's face it, will probably never see. Things like this…" She traced a pansy with her fingertip before she looked up. A world of truth showed in her gaze, and Pansy didn't try to deny what she saw or what had been said. It would be a disservice to them both if she did, so she kept quiet.

They sat in silence for several minutes, each lost in her musings. Pansy imagined her friend thought of their differences, while she considered their similarities. Both had strong family ties and feelings of commitment. Bess wouldn't leave her mother, not as long as she thought she needed her, despite her own love for Todd. And Pansy hadn't been able to leave her hometown before taking care of her parents' final affairs, even though she'd wanted to leave on the first train out of town. And both women wanted to find their way to a happy life, filled with love and laughter.

She turned to Bess and put a hand over the one that lay on top of the tea towel. A gentle squeeze to reassure. "We aren't that different, my friend. We may come from different backgrounds, but our beginnings have led us here. To this moment, when we both can choose how to move forward with our lives."

A head shake sent a lock of hair tumbling to hang beside a rosy cheek. "I don't have any choices, Pansy. Until Mama decides to move in with Aunt Myra, I can't leave her. And I can't stop doin' what I'm doin', no matter how much I hate it. I have to help my mother." She shrugged, then lifted her gaze. A tiny smile touched her lips. "And I guess that's my choice, isn't it?"

She couldn't think of a way to dispute that logic, so Pansy nodded. Sadness for the other's lot in life swept through her. Embarrassment at her own naivete warmed her cheeks. Bess wasn't able to make her own decisions, not if she wanted to continue to support her mother. That she'd thought herself in a similar situation brought embarrassment, and regret. How could she ever have been so childish?

Bess handed the tea towel back with a smile. "It's not finished."

Puzzled, she looked down at it. It certainly seemed complete. "Did you want another flower? Or a spray of greenery near the center?" She couldn't see where it lacked, but would gladly add whatever would make her friend happy.

"No, nothing like that. It needs your signature. Well, your initials, at least."

"My initials?" Pansy searched the other's eyes for a clue that she joked, but there wasn't a hint of teasing. "Whatever for?"

"Because that, Miss Priscilla Buchanan, is a work of art. I mayn't have been to any high-falootin' museums or slick cities, but I know art when it's starin' me in the face." She stood, wiped a hand down the front of her apron, and set her empty mug on the bench. "Now why don't you add the final touch while I take that washing down? I've got soup on for supper. We've got just enough time to eat before I have to get ready for...well, for later on."

As she walked across the yard, Pansy's gaze followed. Her new friend showed so much determination and devotion it was admirable. Despite her feelings for

Todd, she did what needed doing and never complained. Even now, she folded sheets and towels with a smile, then set them in the basket that sat beneath the tree at the far end of the wash line.

Pansy used the length of deep green thread hanging from her needle to hurriedly sign the tea towel. She wove the end of the thread beneath the stitches of the nearest bunch of flowers, then bit the needle free with her teeth. She stood and hurried over to help fold the largest sheet, dropping the towel on the edge of the basket.

"Let me get these corners." She grabbed one end, and they each took a few steps backward, pulling the fabric taut. "It's easier with an extra set of hands."

Bess smiled. "Most things are."

****

Clive hadn't met many people in Wylder, but the ones he'd become acquainted with were good folks. Hard-working, honest, and as friendly as any he'd ever met. Most were making the best of the hard life they had, for whatever reason, chosen. Nothing fancy about them, no hoity-toity airs. Oh, sure, there were a few women who paraded down Wylder Street as if they were still back east, or at least wishing they were, but even most of them had a nod or smile for a passing stranger.

He liked that. Folks who welcomed others without having to know all their business first. His life was not an open book, ready for perusal by every Nosey Nellie he met. And he'd met a number of those in his time, but not, thankfully, here in Wylder.

He'd been in town long enough for some of the faces to be familiar. When he saw one of his favorite people, the town undertaker, walking toward him, he smiled. The man reminded him of his brother Owen. A strong yet humble demeanor, a man who spoke from the heart with a look in his eyes that invited trust and made it clear that his word was his bond. The type of man he'd follow into a gunfight or battle without a second thought.

"Good to see you again, Gus."

The undertaker touched the brim of his hat with a hand and gave a nod. A slow smile spread across his face. "That's a two-way trail. I'm glad you're sticking around town for a bit, and not just passin' through." The man's accent gave a depth to his words.

"Well, I guess Wylder's growin' on me." They stood near the telegraph office, down by the railroad depot. He'd been thinking to send a wire to his brother, to let him know he'd decided to linger in the west a bit. When a man didn't have a lot of family, it didn't do to cause those kin he did have any worry. He let his gaze travel over the wood-frame buildings. They were sturdy, even though most lacked paint or fine architectural details. Didn't seem to matter none or take away from the rugged beauty of the town.

"Are you thinking you might settle here with us? I can tell you this is a good place to plant some roots." The other man sounded hopeful. A few days ago, he'd shared that he had worried he might not be welcome in town, given his occupation and all, but he'd quickly seen that his fears were unfounded. "Like I said the other night, Wylder welcomed me. Good people here, a good place to settle and have a family."

Yes. A family. Exactly what Clive hadn't realized he'd wanted—until recently.

"I remember. And I've been thinking on it."

Movement on the depot platform caught his attention. If he wasn't mistaken—and he knew he wasn't the minute his gaze fell on the figure's womanly curves—Miss Buchanan had business at the depot. Strange, to be about the place at this time of day. The next train wouldn't stop in Wylder for two days. Did she plan to be on it when it pulled out and headed west?

He had to know. While he'd planned to send a message to his brother, then invite Gus to the Five Star to chat some more over a glass of whiskey, the appearance of the woman changed things.

A smile to show his apology for cutting their conversation short. "I see someone I need to speak with." He tipped his head toward the train station. The woman had walked around the building and could not be seen, but the undertaker didn't glance that way, anyhow. Nice to meet someone who knew better than to show too much curiosity. "If you'll excuse me…"

A head nod and another slow smile. "Of course. I'm sure we'll see each other around town again."

"I'm sure." He touched the brim of his hat, then headed toward the depot.

Small talk could wait. The woman could not.

****

Pansy cupped her hands and pressed her forehead against the tiny square of glass. She had been checking on her trunk every day, just to be certain it remained secure in the railroad depot storage room. In the days since Hosa told her he'd left it waiting for her, she had worried it would disappear. But it hadn't, and today, much to her relief, there were other trunks stowed in the room with hers. A few hat boxes and some wooden boxes, as well.

Well, that brought some ease to her mind. Experience had taught her that it would last until this time tomorrow, when she would have to find an excuse to get out of the house and come check again. She had no idea what she would do if she peeked in the window and saw an empty room. All of her belongings were in that trunk. Her identity, the person she once was, at the very least, tied to the bits and bobs packed within its sturdy walls. It felt like ages ago she'd considered every item, packing each with so much care. To lose it all now…well, she just couldn't stand the thought. The very idea turned her legs to water.

She turned on one heel and leaned her back against the wooden siding. She had pushed a narrow crate beneath the tiny window, the way she'd done every evening. It had hardly enough room for her to plant both feet on, and none for a misstep. It wouldn't take much to send her tottering off and onto the unforgiving wooden platform, so she took care. The last thing she needed to top this tangled mess of a life she'd found, a broken bone.

No thanks, she'd pass on breaking herself. She took a deep breath and hiked the edge of her skirt high enough that she could put a foot down without becoming entangled. Just as she shifted her weight, she heard a familiar voice.

"Need a hand?"

Pansy looked up as she lost her balance and flew out into the space above the hard walkway. She dropped her skirt, her arms windmilled, and much to her chagrin, she let out a squeak that sounded as if she'd stepped on a mouse.

Clive's arms shot out, and she landed in a heap against his chest. His warm breath brushed her cheek, and the gaze in his eyes when she looked up at him sent her blood simmering. Lord, but the man could turn her inside out!

"What—" A length of hair hung in her eyes, so she blew it to one side. It dangled near her cheek, but she didn't brush it away. Her hands were on the man's shoulders, and he held her as easily as if she were a sack of feathers. A nice arrangement, one she wasn't quick to end. "What are you doing here, sneaking up on me like that?"

One corner of his upper lip lifted, and her heart flip-flopped in her chest.

"I did not sneak up on you. I merely happened along while you were busy…" The lip went higher. "What were you doing, exactly? I mean, you were so engaged that you didn't hear me walk up behind you."

She swallowed, reaching for the hair and pushing it back in place. The maneuver bought her a minute to think, but no more. How to explain her actions, especially when she'd been caught in the act of spying?

Did it count as spying if you were only watching a piece of luggage? She wasn't sure, but either way, she looked guilty, and she knew it.

Time to turn the tables. Even if her heart urged her to tell the man anything he asked.

"Why are you still in Wylder?"

Clive pushed the brim of his hat back a tad, exposing more of the face that had been invading her dreams the past few nights. How the man had gotten under her skin, she still didn't know. The only thing she knew for certain, that he intrigued her like no other ever had.

"Well, maybe I'm thinking of settlin' down here. Seems like as good a place as any." He grinned, sending her insides tumbling. "And folks are friendly. I like that about a place." His head turned, and he surveyed the little bit of town they could see from their vantage point. Then, he returned his attention to her. "What about you, Miss Buchanan? Are you looking for friendly folks and peaceful days? Seems to me that Wylder is that kind of welcoming place, don't it?"

She couldn't argue with him, because she agreed. Wylder felt like the ideal spot to settle down. The only sticking point, that if she did decide to stay, she would have to come clean with her sisters about not telling them when she arrived. She doubted they would look favorably on her hiding from them. Lily, especially, might show her persnickety, eldest-sister side.

Mother had been right when she'd said that keeping the truth hidden wouldn't ever bring about favorable results. A good thing she couldn't see how her youngest disregarded her teaching, Pansy thought.

"It does seem like a fine spot to live." She tilted her head to the side and raised a hand to shadow her eyes. The sun behind him put his face in shadow. "Honestly, it's the nicest frontier town I've seen so far."

A chuckle sent tremors along her skin. Little jolts of pleasure, bringing a smile she couldn't stop.

"Better'n Chicago, then?"

Pansy laughed. "Yes, definitely better than Chicago!"

The man took a step to the side, blocking the sun with his head, so she dropped her hand. He'd only been in shadow for a few minutes, yet the reemergence of his features brought unexpected joy.

I have lost my mind. Over a man, no less!

He held out an arm, bent at the elbow, and dipped his chin. "Would you do me the honor of walking a little way with me? I hear the path to the cemetery is a pretty one, lined with wildflowers and such. That is, unless your business here isn't finished."

What could it hurt to walk a while with him?

She took his arm. "I'd like that, Mr. Cooper."

Chapter 10

Dinners with Sandy and Bess were simple affairs. There were none of the flashy table settings that accompanied the meals her previous life held. Table linens were kept in a cupboard, if the pair even owned any, and meals were served from the stove onto plates, so there were no serving dishes to pass. Clearing away and washing up went quickly.

Most evenings they talked about ordinary topics, like the weather or tomorrow's chore list. Nothing earth-shattering, but enough that the meals passed with companionable conversation.

Not this meal, though. A tension in the air hovered just above the table itself, like a dark rain cloud ready to send a torrent down on them. Pansy had heard the mother and daughter bickering earlier and assumed that dissent caused this change in atmosphere.

She was happy when the last bit of potato and mouthful of cornbread had been swallowed. Her body practically jumped from her chair in a rush to clear the table.

Sandy left the two younger women to the after-dinner tasks, the same as always. Tonight, there wasn't a flurry of chatter from Bess, even with her mother gone from the room. Pansy didn't push her to talk. Living with so many sisters had taught her to wait for a story to unfold and a person to share their burdens.

As Pansy dried the last plate and stacked it on the others stored on an open shelf, she glanced over at Bess. The young woman had hardly said a word since dinner, and her eyes were pink and red-rimmed.

Another spat with Todd likely caused this much despair. She doubted the scuffle with Sandy could bring this amount of discontent. After all, the pair argued about Sandy moving in with her sister Myra at least once a day. This had to be more.

Pansy searched for something to say as she folded the dish towel and hung it to dry. She considered a number of opening lines designed to encourage confidences but dismissed them all. Better to get straight to the heart of things and hope their talk might give her new friend some relief.

"Bess, did something happen between this morning and now? You were so lighthearted then, and now you seem mighty low." She put a hand on the other's shoulder and gave a small squeeze before she let go. "Do you want to talk about it?"

A fast glance at the doorway leading to the front of the house, before Bess nodded to the back door. She walked out, and Pansy followed. When the door shut behind them, they walked to the far end of the porch, away from the doorway. It became clear that Bess didn't want her mother to overhear the conversation.

"Todd." The word came out on a sigh. "We had another argument."

As she'd suspected. Love shouldn't come at such a dear price. To sacrifice contentment for another didn't seem to be a wise idea. From what she could tell, Bess suffered more than she should—more than anyone in love should.

But how to show someone else, especially a person in the throes of romance, that the situation they currently occupied damaged them?

Bess' eyes showed clearly that she endured heartache over this latest disagreement. The darkness could not hide her emotions, although she put on a good effort to control herself. Crossed arms, almost as if she hugged herself to keep from crying, broke Pansy's heart. One thing to know someone hurt and quite another to actually witness their despair.

She wanted to gather her friend close and hug her tight but knew from experience with her sisters that it might send the other into a fresh wave of tears, so she held back. Instead, she placed a gentle hand on the other's shoulder again and left it there.

"I'm so sorry you and Todd are having such a hard time of it. Do you think…" She swallowed, trying to find a kind way to phrase what she had in her mind.

Bess saved her from articulating. A fast head shake to deny what she must have seen coming. "No, I don't think we should end things. We love each other. I might not know everything, but I am certain of that." She scrubbed a palm across a cheek when a tear slid down. "That's what we argue about, really. We want to be together, but as long as Mama refuses to leave this place—" She turned so forcefully that Pansy's hand came off her shoulder. Bess waved a closed fist at the house behind them. "As long as she won't leave here, I can't begin the life with Todd we both dream of. It's so ridiculous. Mama and Aunt Myra could be happy in the other house, and no one would have to worry about keeping this one up. And Todd and I could be married, and begin a family, and…" A low wail, the sound so like a wounded animal it sent gooseflesh rising on Pansy's arms, finished for her.

Pansy took a step forward and pulled her friend into her arms. The other's trembling increased as she succumbed to the tears she'd been holding at bay. Pansy held her, letting her cry and hoping that somehow, some way, Bess and Todd would find their way to their happy future together.

When Bess' tears had lessened to small hiccups and sniffles, she guided the other woman to the back door and into the house. There wasn't any need to speak, and, really, what could she say? No words could comfort at this point, but she hoped that a good nights' sleep would bring a lighter mood.

Pansy turned to lock the back door as Bess headed upstairs. She spotted the dry laundry hanging on the lines and two baskets of folded, clean clothing on the porch steps. She and Bess had meant to bring it all inside earlier but had been caught up doing other things. Now, it would wait until tomorrow.

She turned the knob on the dead bolt and sighed.

Tomorrow. One small word that carried so much weight. Hopes, dreams, promises…and uncertainty.

****

"But, Pansy, you must have known all along that Filbert Snowe wasn't the man for you." Emmaline tossed one of her blonde curls over her shoulder and waved a dramatic hand through the air. "I mean, he's nice and all, but that's not enough for you. You need a man with a dash of excitement, one who makes your heart jump when he walks into a room. Good old Filly won't ever do that to you, no matter how much he tries."

They were seated side by side on a bench in the park

they'd visited since they were babies being pushed in carriages by their mothers. The air, so warm and lilac scented, washed over her. Sunbeams danced on the path at their feet, and birdsong filled the air.

Pansy settled back against the bench, even though she knew Mother would expect her to maintain a ladylike posture. She didn't care. Her spine rounded a bit as she gazed around them, contentment filling her as smoothly as raindrops fill a barrel.

"Oh, he tries, in his own way." She had to give Filly that. He did his best to make her happy. Unfortunately, his idea of what they needed didn't coincide with the vision she had for her future. "And he's here, Emmaline. My parents expect us to wed. You know they've pretty much made that decision for me."

Another truth. And just one more example of how Mother and Father decided her future, as if she wasn't wise enough to determine the path of her own life.

"Isn't this journey all about making your own decisions? Ones not based on resisting what everyone else has in mind for you, but finding out exactly what you want for yourself?"

She gave her friend a small smile.

"You're like one of those wise owls in the picture books we used to read when we were children. How can you know so much?"

Emmaline shook her head, sending the cascade of golden curls swishing across her shoulders. "I don't know anything that you don't already know. You have to admit that Mr. Snowe is cold as ice, and not for you. You need someone fiery, like that handsome Clive Cooper."

Clive Cooper. Just the thought of the man sent Pansy's heart stuttering in her chest.

"What do you know about Clive?"

The other's laughter filled the air. A shrill sound, not at all like the typical musical twitter she had cultivated. The birdsong seemed louder, too. Harsher and stringent.

"Oh, I know more than you think I do, Pansy. After all, we are best friends…"

The scent of lilacs soured as loud banging cut through the chirping birds and laughter.

She sucked in a breath, but it didn't come easily.

"Someone fiery, that's what you need!"

Emmaline's words turned harsh.

"Fiery, Pansy. Fiery—"

She woke to the sound of banging and the taste of smoke. A fast breath sent her into a fit of coughing. Her eyes watered as they flew open. In the darkness, a red glow danced across the ceiling, brought in through the open window to light the room.

Oh, dear Lord, the house was on fire!

Pansy's feet hit the floor fast. One toe caught in the hem of her nightgown, and she stumbled before finding her balance. Fear turned her legs wobbly, but she put a hand over her mouth and willed herself to move toward the bedroom door. In the small room she crossed the space in a few steps, grabbed the wrought-iron handle, and yanked the door open. A cloud of acrid smoke swirled around her.

The narrow hallway stood dark, every bit of light swallowed by the menacing smoke. She put a hand on the wall, hoping to find her way to the staircase. Here, sounds reached her ears that she hadn't heard in her bedroom. Stomping feet and frantic yells.

Her name. A voice she recognized. "Priscilla!" The

sound of bootheels on the wooden stair treads. "Priscilla Buchanan—can you hear me?"

She opened her mouth to speak but swallowed smoke. Coughing, harder now than a few minutes ago, brought her to her knees.

Out of the darkness, denim-covered legs appeared. Strong hands lifted her to her feet.

"We need to get you out of here." When Clive Cooper pulled her against his chest, she pressed her face to the cotton shirt covering his broad chest and took a deep inhale. The scent of him filled her head and for a moment blocked out the horror that surrounded them. He took a step back, and she tilted her head to meet his gaze. "Can you walk?"

She nodded. When he took her hand and headed for the stairs, she followed with her face as close to his back as possible. His body blocked some of the smoke that rushed up the stairs. When they reached the bottom, he loosened his hold and pushed her ahead of him toward the kitchen.

Pansy expected to find the fire in the kitchen, but there weren't any flames. More smoke, certainly, but no active fire. A surprise that she didn't have time to consider. The back door stood open, and she ran for it.

Fresh air hit her like a cooling wave, but she didn't have time to stand in relief. To the right, at the far end of the porch, flames licked their way across the wooden support column. She glanced down at the railing. Most of it had burned away, along with the column closest to the exterior wall of the house. The porch roof sagged, dripping embers on the men below who were, even as she ran past, throwing water from buckets at the blaze.

Bess and Sandy stood near one of the trees beyond

the wash lines. There, too, signs of the fire showed. Blackened laundry and singed sheets waved in the warm breeze.

"I'm so glad you're out!" Bess pulled her in for a fast hug. "I called for you, but you didn't answer. And then the sheriff burst in and pulled me and Mama out so fast my head about spun."

Sandy stepped forward and ran a hand down Pansy's arm. "I'm so sorry this happened." She turned to the house and gave a sniff. "I fear we may lose everythin' to the fire."

It hit Pansy then that she had run out without her carpetbag. All her most treasured possessions were in that bag—painted miniatures of her parents, the letters her sisters had written, everything she'd brought west to begin her new life…

A stone bit into the heel of her foot when she turned and headed toward the burning house. She had to get back inside, had to get the bag and its contents safely outdoors. The thought that she might never see the miniatures again brought bile up her throat, and for an instant she fought to not embarrass herself. She swallowed hard and took another step.

"Pansy!" A familiar voice cut through the cacophony surrounding her. "Pansy Bloom!"

There had never been one day in her life when she didn't welcome the sound of her sister Daisy's voice. Of all her sisters, Daisy was the one who bossed her around the least. Maybe because the author had a free spirit and had always been fiercely independent, she encouraged her youngest sister to press for a bit of freedom herself. In any case, when Pansy heard her name called, she knew instantly who had spotted her.

She stopped and began to turn back toward the crowd near the trees and fence. A familiar figure ran up to her. With her curls flying wildly and a blanket thrown loosely over her nightdress, her sister looked like a figure from a child's picture book. But when she grabbed Pansy's shoulders and pulled her into a crushing embrace, there wasn't any doubt she was real.

"Good Lord, Pansy—whatever are you doing in Wylder? Why are you here? I've written you so many letters these past weeks, and you haven't answered!" Daisy pushed her away and held her at arm's length. The stare in her eyes showed both relief and annoyance. A typical Daisy expression, it brought Pansy's mind off her belongings still in the house, but only for a moment. "Addison said he'd go to Charleston to find you and was planning to leave next week—and here you are. What's going on?"

She tugged against her sister's grip. Explanations could come later. Now, she had to retrieve her bag before the fire claimed it.

"Let me go!" Daisy's grip didn't loosen, so she pulled harder. "Daisy, let me go! My bag is in the house—all my important things, they'll be lost—"

Her sister's grip tightened. When she shook her head, her hair flew, ringlets outlined momentarily against the glare of the fire behind her.

"I won't let you go back in there. I don't care what you left inside. It's not nearly as important as you are!"

"Mother and Father—their miniatures. They're in my bag." She gasped as tears slipped from her eyes. "I can't lose them again, I just can't!"

Shock showed on the other's face, but her fingers held tightly. They bit into the skin on Pansy's upper arms, capturing her in a hold that she couldn't escape.

Violet appeared, a vision in the darkness. Beside her, a Chinese woman.

"Pansy!" She turned to Daisy, then leveled her gaze on Pansy again. "What's going on? Dear sister, when did you get to Wylder?"

When her schoolteacher sister pulled her into her arms, Pansy did not resist. By now, her belongings must be gone. The new life plan she'd tried so hard to build for herself might as well be swallowed by smoke, too. Defeat brought down the last barrier between her and the tears that threatened.

Violet's arms tightened around her as Pansy let the sobs come. Daisy's arms wrapped around her, too. The long curls draped over her shoulder as her sister tucked her chin over her head.

She cried, then. Tears fell so hard and fast that she didn't stop to consider what she cried over. Loss, certainly. Her parents, the way of life she'd known, the opportunity to choose her path in the world, the knowledge that she'd gladly give up choosing if she could have her parents back. Defeat. She'd tried so hard to make good decisions, worked tirelessly to build options for herself—and for what? To lose every inch she'd gained? It hardly seemed fair.

Violet's voice, a soft murmur above her head. "Oh, Lily, it's our beautiful Pansy."

Another pair of arms circled them, insulating her from everything that this horrid night offered. She breathed in the love of her sisters and heard Father's voice in her head. He'd given them each the middle name Mae, and never missed an opportunity to remind them that he'd done so for a reason.

"My beautiful Bloom girls—may they always know the love they share makes them the most loving garden on earth—wise Lily Mae, headstrong Daisy Mae, practical Violet Mae, and our littlest, wildest flower, Pansy Mae."

****

Two days had passed since the fire.

Pansy didn't argue when her sisters demanded she leave with them. Violet took her home to her tidy little lavender house. Lily and Daisy came along, too, and together the trio insisted she take a nice, long, bubble bath in a big tin tub in Violet's kitchen. Along with Lin, the Chinese woman who lived with Violet, they cared for her as if she were still a little girl. Even with freshly washed, combed, and braided hair, a clean nightdress, and tucked into a comfortable bed in the guestroom, she couldn't stop her tears. But when Daisy crawled on top of the bedcovers and wrapped an arm around her while the other two watched from the other bed in the cozy room, she finally found peace. It was as if they were children again, beneath their parents' roof, safe and secure.

That first night, there were nightmares. Smoke and fire-filled dreams woke her, but each time her eyes flew open, a sister whispered words of safety. For two days, the sisters lived together in the small home with Lin. Then Lily and Daisy returned to their own homes, leaving three to settle into a routine in the schoolteacher's comfortable residence.

At first, Pansy missed the other two sisters. No one had pressured her to explain her presence. They had all been welcoming, loving, and sisterly. They supported her when she began to tell them of what brought her west, seemingly content to let her tell the story in her way, in her time. She appreciated that consideration.

Clive Cooper had called nearly every afternoon. The first day, he'd returned her precious bag. It reeked of smoke, but it and its contents were unharmed. He'd explained that the fire had started in a laundry basket on the porch. Apparently, Todd had been standing in the shadows, smoking a cigar and considering how to convince Bess to marry him. He'd come from the Five Star, where whiskey colored his thinking, and flicked ashes in the basket, thinking to only frighten Bess' mother enough that she would consent to move.

But the small fire grew quickly, making Todd holler for help. He'd run inside, thinking to grab Bess and Sandy and lead them to safety, but he'd, in his drunken state, stumbled. The sheriff found him and rescued him as well as the two women. The lawman was about to go in for Pansy when Clive arrived, pushed him aside, and rushed in.

It was a miracle they were all alive.

Another miracle that the house hadn't burned to the ground. The men of Wylder had been fast to react, and while the porch had burned, the remainder of the house still stood. Uninhabitable for the foreseeable future, given its dousing with water and the lingering stink of smoke.

Bess and Sandy had moved in with Myra. And Pansy? She mulled over her future some but didn't let it consume her.

Instead, she focused on being grateful to not have succumbed to the smoke that filled her room that fateful night.

And she enjoyed spending time with Clive. His daily

visits were the high point of her days now.

She closed her eyes and rested her head against the back of the chair. She'd taken to sitting on Violet's back porch in a wide, comfortable chair that had a seat made for relaxing. Chickadees danced in the trees beyond the railing. A ginger cat lay on the bottom step, eyes closed and as motionless as a statue.

A knock sounded at the front door. The house wasn't large enough that she didn't hear it. No need to rush to answer it, though. Lin spent most afternoons reading in the front room, working on increasing her English language skills. Surely, she would get the door.

Bootheels rapped against floorboards, coming closer with each step. A smile played around the edges of Pansy's lips. The man made her happy, and there wasn't any sense trying to claim it wasn't so. The hinges on the door creaked as he came through, so she opened her eyes and looked over her shoulder.

Lord, but the man made her heart beat fast!

He hadn't minded when she told him her truth. She had expected he would be angry, the way Filly would have been, but he'd merely accepted her explanation. Then, they moved on.

But that didn't mean he didn't take the chance to gently tease her when he thought to do so.

"Why, good afternoon, Miss Buchanan." His voice washed over her, a warm, comforting wave that offered security she hadn't felt since before her parents took ill and passed. The words came with a crooked smile. He tipped his head and twirled the hat he held loosely in one hand. "Don't mean to disturb your sleep, but I was wondering if you'd do me the honor of riding down Wylder Street with me. I have a buggy from the livery out front."

Every day he found some new activity to delight her. There had been dinners at the Wylder Hotel, a show at the outdoor theatre, and walks on the boardwalk before sundown. Once, he had taken her riding to visit Lily and Theo at their homestead.

And there had been gifts. Trinkets from the mercantile. Fruit, for her and Violet and Lin, too. A beaded bracelet he'd gotten from a native trading post. And a pair of earbobs. She wore them now.

"A buggy, Mr. Cooper?" She didn't mind teasing him back when she could. "Now, if that doesn't sound fancy, I don't know what does. Whatever are you thinking, taking a buggy from the livery on a pleasant afternoon?" She sat upright and smoothed a hand down the front of her dress. Violet had loaned it to her, saying the color brought out the highlights in Pansy's hair. She hoped that was true, and not just her sister's way of making her feel welcome. "Why, are you unwell? Seems like a strong man such as yourself wouldn't need the services of a buggy…that is, unless something was ailing him."

A head shake sent a lock of hair tumbling across his forehead. When he looked as if he wasn't going to rise to her teasing, she sucked in a breath. He knelt beside her chair, putting them face-to-face. The spicy scent of his aftershave lotion made her lean closer.

"Well, it's like this." He placed an elbow on the arm of her chair and tipped his chin toward his chest. "For a bit I wondered if my head might be in need of some fixing. Addlepated, you know. Just couldn't get my mind off a certain woman." He nodded, as if confirming the issue, and moved an inch closer. "Then, I contemplated seein' Doc about my chest. I kind of had a heavy feeling, right around my heart."

Pansy held the breath. Their teasing had become something new, something with a weight to it. Suddenly, his words mattered more than their usual banter did.

By the look in Clive's eyes, he'd left teasing behind.

Her mouth went dry. Her own chest felt tight as her heart beat faster. And there wasn't anything in the world that could force her to look away.

She had always speculated about how it felt to be held under the spell of a man's gaze. Romance novels made it seem magical, but she had never known for sure.

Until now.

Clive reached out and took her hand in his. He ran a lazy thumb across her knuckles, sending chills dancing along her skin.

"My heart isn't ailing, though. Not my head, either." His words came slowly, as if each one held a wealth of meaning. "You see, that lady who caught my attention also captured my heart. Now, before I met her, I didn't know where I was going or what I planned to do with the rest of my life. I only knew I needed a change." He offered a small smile. "Ever feel that way, like you need a change?"

Pansy nodded. "You know I have. It's what brought me out west."

"And I'm grateful for that." Clive took a deep breath, then let it out in one long, slow exhale. He gave her fingers a gentle squeeze before he went on. She wasn't sure if it was meant to reassure her—or him. "Pansy Bloom, I know most folks would think we haven't properly courted. And I know it might seem crazy, the way I feel and what I'm about to ask, but please believe me, I'm speaking from my heart."

Oh, Lord, the man had definitely left teasing far behind.

"The reason I rented that buggy from the livery is to take you out on a proper ride to see a house I purchased. It's a nice place in town, so it's near two of the Bloom sisters." He paused. Time stood still as she gazed into his eyes. "It's the place I'm hoping this Bloom sister will find nice enough to call her own. Pansy, I fell in love with you the minute we met on that train. I know it's not the most proper courtship, but I can't hold back. I promise, I'll do my best to make you a happy woman. This frontier living isn't what you're used to, but it's as good a place as any for two people to build a life together. Will you marry me?"

They had only known each other for a short time, but she saw forever in his eyes. And that, the promise of a lifetime, brought her to the most important decision she'd ever made.

She'd had enough wild adventures. Too many, really. What she wanted now was to find the same kind of peace and happiness her parents had. And this man, on his knee before her, had already brought her joy and contentment.

"Yes, Clive. I'll marry you!"

His arms went around her as he pulled her close. Clive's lips claimed hers. And in that instant Pansy knew that no matter how long she lived, no moment in time would ever rival this one.

Her parents had always told them that love mattered more than anything else. Her sisters had found their true loves in Wylder. And, despite her thinking she would be the one to decide to roam farther, she had done the same.

As Clive deepened their kiss, a thought swept through Pansy's head.

I've finally found my place in the world.
Wylder, always and forever.

A word about the author...

Sarita Leone loves happy endings—in life and on the page.

When she's not busy writing her next novel, this adventure-loving yoga teacher likes to hike, travel, and dance beneath the stars. She studies languages, enjoys making a mess in the kitchen, and never says "no" to fun.

Finding pockets of peace everywhere she goes, this author plans to make every moment of this journey count.